Alie[?] P9-ECT-178

Arline —
Is this weird
enough for you?

The Council of Love

Leonor Fini

The Council of Love

A Celestial Tragedy in Five Acts

By Oskar Panizza

*Translated from the German
by Oreste F. Pucciani*

Introduction by André Breton

*With five original drawings
by Leonor Fini*

*A Richard Seaver Book
The Viking Press | New York*

Das Liebeskonzil

Published by Verlags-Magazin (J. Schabelitz)

English language translation Copyright © 1973
by Oreste F. Pucciani

Drawings Copyright © 1973 by Lénor Fini

Introduction Copyright © 1960 by André Breton

All rights reserved

A Richard Seaver Book / The Viking Press, Inc.

First published in 1973 in a hardbound
and paperbound edition by The Viking Press, Inc.,
625 Madison Avenue, New York, N.Y. 10022

Published simultaneously in Canada by
The Macmillan Company of Canada Limited

SBN 670-24404-x (hardbound)

    670-00403-0 (paperbound)

Library of Congress catalog card number: 73-2498

All the photographs in the present volume are
from the Paris production
and were taken by Nicolas Treatt.

Used by permission of the photographer.

Printed in U.S.A.

To the memory of

Ulrich von Hutten

It has pleased God in our time to send illnesses (as it behooves us to notice) which were unknown to our forefathers. Thus say those charged with the defense of Holy Scripture that syphilis came from God's wrath and that so does God punish and afflict our evil ways.

—*Ulrich von Hutten, a Teutonic Knight,*
Of the French Illness or Syphilis, *1519*

Dic Dea, quae causae nobis post saecula tanta insolitam peperere luem? . . .

—*Fracastoro,* Syphilis sive de morbo gallico, *1530*

$\mathfrak{T}$RANSLATOR'S $\mathfrak{P}$REFACE

Oskar Panizza (1853–1921) wrote *The Council of Love* in the spring of 1893. It was published in Zurich in October 1894. In spite of the fact that the play was not published in Germany, the Bavarian authorities took immediate steps against *The Council of Love*, and on April 30, 1895, Panizza was condemned to one year of imprisonment. He served his sentence from 1895 to 1896 in the prison of Amberg. After his release he settled in Zurich, where he remained until 1898. In the fall of 1898 he was expelled from Zurich for having had relations with a prostitute who was under fifteen years of age. He fled to Paris, where he remained until April 1901. It was at this time that the Court of Munich issued an order for his arrest because of poems that Panizza had published while in Paris, *Parisiana* (December 1899), attacking Emperor William II. Panizza was obliged to return to Germany because the government had confiscated his property, and he was arrested and sent to the insane asylum of Upper Bavaria. He was kept there, "under observation," for six weeks.

After his release no further legal action was taken against him, and Panizza returned to Paris. In November 1903 he began to manifest signs of the paranoia for which he was to be confined for the rest of his life. Convinced that he was being persecuted by agents of the German government in Paris, Panizza complained of hearing repeated blasts from a whistle calculated to destroy his nerves, of finding that his door locks had been tampered with, his fires put out, his water supply cut off. On July 23, 1904, Panizza left for Lausanne, whence he returned to Munich and took refuge in the private asylum of Neufriedenheim. Expelled by the director, Dr. Rehm, Panizza rented a private room and lived for a while in seclusion. On October 9 he unsuccessfully attempted suicide in the Jardin Anglais of the city. Seeking arrest and confinement, as he tells it in his autobiography, he went out into the streets on October 19, 1904, dressed only in a shirt, and succeeded in getting himself arrested. He was taken to the municipal hospital. In February 1905 he was sent to the Herzogshöhe sanitarium in Bayreuth, where he remained until his death. He did not even know that war broke out in 1914.

Panizza has remained virtually unknown until the present time. Scarcely a dozen articles dealing with him and his work appeared between 1919 and 1951. In 1951 Walter Mehring's *The Lost Library* (published by Bobbs Merrill) devoted a number of eloquent pages to Panizza, and it was in the French translation of this work that Jean Brejoux discovered him. Brejoux's translation, *Le Concile d'amour*, with a preface by André Breton, appeared in the collection "Libertés" by Jean-Jacques Pauvert

(Paris) in 1964. Also in 1964 a German edition of Panizza's works appeared: *Das Liebeskonzil und Andere Schriften* (H. Lachterhand Verlag). The recent brilliant production at the Théâtre de Paris by Jorge Lavelli· and Leonor Fini is responsible for the present interest in the works of Panizza, and especially in *The Council of Love.*

The play is, in the words of Panizza, "A Celestial Tragedy." It is a modern mystery play which takes place in Heaven, Hell, and at the Court of Pope Alexander VI in the year 1495, the first recorded date of the outbreak of syphilis in the Western world. The main characters of the play are, as might be expected, God, the Virgin Mary, Jesus, the Devil, and the "Woman," Syphilis. The argument of the play is simple: Humanity is out of control; lust and pleasure know no bounds; Heaven, to whom this state of affairs is revealed by a special messenger from Naples, becomes alarmed. How is it to maintain its supremacy? God, Who is omnipotent, could of course destroy the world, but then there would be no men, and Heaven needs mankind. Perhaps God should create something new, as He had once done. The difficulty is that God is old and His creative ability virtually exhausted. The Divinity is, in fact, in such a state of decrepitude that He can barely maintain the normal, daily status of the world. Meanwhile, neither Mary nor Jesus possesses the creative gift. Mary, in fact, is more human than divine, and Jesus is a dull fanatic, sick and ailing, tired of his role of savior. After viewing the excesses of the Pope's Court, which are shown to us in brilliant detail, the divinities decide that only their old accomplice and victim can do the trick. There must be a "Council of Love," where Satan's advice is sought.

Satan is, as André Breton said, *sympathique*. But he is more than that: He is an intellectual and a revolutionary, a genius who alone threatened the established order of Heaven and who, long ages ago, forced the Divinity to a compromise and to a division of the world's goods. Yet, in his princely banishment, he knows a gnawing nostalgia for the fine world, grand manners, and aristocratic opulence of Heaven. When his foot aches—he injured it in his Fall—he thinks of the great people whom he forsook and dreams of social promotion.

It is no easy matter to deal with Satan, and God almost muffs it. God can be very insulting. Fortunately, there is Jesus, who can double-talk, and there is Mary, who has a womanly instinct both for her own grandeur and for offended sensibilities. She manages where God fails, and succeeds in enlisting the aid of Satan in a difficult enterprise. Something must be invented: a good old-fashioned sort of punishment. It must be a plague to mankind and yet leave the soul intact; there must be suffering as a consequence of evil deeds, and yet the possibility of redemption must remain. Even Satan finds the task difficult. But he is a genius and has an idea. Returning to Hell, he calls up the celebrated female sinners of the past: Helen of Troy, Phryne, Héloïse, Agrippina. None will do until he reaches Salome. Then he knows he has found his answer. Only Salome was capable of indifference and true pleasure in the commission of evil. With Salome he will have a child. A child whom he will be able to present at court: the loveliest child in the world who will poison all of mankind. Perhaps with Syphilis he will even gain his "freedom of thought."

But is *The Council of Love* really a play about syphilis? The answer, as Breton perceived, is that it is not, but is about human freedom and about evil; as such, it prefigured, long before Sartre, the theme of "Nausea." This was the ultimate and occult reason for the persecution of Panizza in his time by a corrupt society that used blasphemy as a pretext and a screen. The ancient Augustinian position that evil has no being emerges in Panizza's play for what it is: an outrageous apology for the existence of evil. Meanwhile a Church-State, which did not even respect international boundaries when it was bent on pious persecution, knew itself to be threatened and subtly denounced in a work that dared to portray the infernal complicity of Heaven and Hell. Banished from the official literature of his time, like the *poètes maudits* of France, Panizza fascinates us, now that he is allowed to emerge, with "a celestial tragedy" of universal appeal.

O.F.P.

CONTENTS

INTRODUCTION

by André Breton

When one ponders the problem of Evil, looking down into
the abyss that Evil is, the rope that men extend to one
another in order to descend into it, and hopefully to climb
out again, suddenly seems dangerously fragile. To touch the
bottom of such an abyss is never anything more than to
make contact with its oozing slime and to experience its
horror without ever being able, by the light of some
flickering lamp, either to assign it limits or, unless one has
recourse to some specious device, to become convinced of its
necessity. This device is to be found in the teaching of the
idea of Sin, whether original or not, and there must always
be cause for surprise and grief in the fact that this should be
commonly considered allowable and sufficient reason in
spite of the outrageous iniquity that it allows to stand: the
monstrous disproportion between, on one hand, an alleged
crime rooted in time immemorial, in myth, ultimately in the
indeterminable (a consequence of symbolic ambiguity), and,
on the other hand, its repression in the guise of the worst
physical and other punishments inflicted upon all of
humanity without discernment and beyond appeal. This
taste for mindless and irresponsible vendetta assuredly could
find no more zealous apologists than the ministers of a
religion which has tended more and more to see in its God
an instrument for its tortures, attributing to the latter an

exemplary sense of "atonement" and to disaster a sense of "testing" which arbitrarily we are asked to take as a sign of divine solicitude.

The bottom of the abyss: why Evil? . . . United in this questioning, which rises from among them like whirlwinds of fire and blazing matter, they are all there, all the Greats—from either side—all those who have been plunged into it, whether against all odds they brought back with them full flowering branches (love rather than the understanding of life), or whether a single branch no less beautiful for being charred. There were those who were plunged there by the tyranny of dogma that enjoined them to go see for themselves and, whatever the cost, to produce a solution that would be binding on their own conscience. Others were appalled from the start by the hideousness of an Evil intended to be a condition of life, and so were set forever against a dogma that lays claim to grounding human freedom in the existence of such an Evil reflected in us and thus finds a way to justify it. Nor were these necessarily the least gallant souls. Between the former and the latter only a narrow mind would attempt to impose an order of precedence. It has always been the same thundercloud shot through with lightning that has brought us, in their time, Dante and Milton, Bosch and Swift, certain of the Gnostics, Gilles de Retz and Sade, Lewis and Maturin, Goethe of the second *Faust* and Hugo of the later poems, Lequier, Nietzsche, Baudelaire, Lautréamont, Rimbaud. Poetry, which indiscriminately favors all of them, does not permit us to separate their voices as they rise to storm pitch. Before we can think of recovering ourselves, before there can be any question of our falling back to our previous positions, they hurl us headlong into the essential drama.

On this ship tossed by the heaviest seas, where the darkest

waves are not the least resplendent, the time has now come to recognize Oscar Panizza. When due allowance is made for the musical score that is being played, the orchestra which concerns us here is not without requiring a certain shrillness of which his instrument alone is capable. Facing Evil and the attempt to justify it by theology, Sade and Lautréamont exalt man in revolt, using sexual and intellectual erethism in all directions as a means for dissipating deceit and for shattering age-old conventions. Curses and defiance are their principal tools, humor being for them only a last resort when the extreme tension that they require of us might cause us to break. On the contrary, with Panizza—much more than with his compatriot Christian Dietrich Grabbe—it is mockery that runs the show where halos fly off all at once and all together in a single, salty gust of wind. From the start his mockery attacks those personifications of the "sacred" which many of our contemporaries continue bent on worshiping, few in number being those among nonbelievers who feel at all compelled to transgress this taboo. In the defense that he will make before the Royal Tribunal of Munich, the author of *The Council of Love* will argue in vain the authority of precedents in this field; the major complaint will stand: that of his having been gifted with greater resources and of having gone infinitely further than any of his predecessors. Indeed, we must acknowledge that the spirit of sedition is brought by him to such a pitch and so bluntly, and treats forbidden things with such insolence that, even today, it is likely that the reaction of an audience would require the curtain to be rung down before the end of the first scene.

The discovery of genius, of such a nature as to emotionalize the entire atmosphere, stems here from the location of the ultrasensitive point from which it becomes possible to bring into play—close enough to ourselves in time so that we are able to feel somewhat involved—the "cause and effect" relationship, given as established by religion, between man's sin and divine wrath expressed in the form of pestilence unleashed over the earth. The fact also that love is *par excellence* the means for man's redemption from the misery of his condition made it of poignant interest to situate the action precisely at that point where, according to the testimony of the chroniclers, the prosecution of heavenly justice was said to have attacked love in order to defile it. It was eminently tempting, using human motives (the only ones we can grasp) to disentangle—both in the upper and lower (?) regions—the threads with which such abominable machinations could have been spun. It is quite probable that desire and pleasure are far from being all of love, and that if man gives them full license, he may well alienate his love as sole principle of transmutation and key to the miraculous. Nonetheless, desire and pleasure are integral parts of love; nothing can prevent flesh from being *one,* and when laws are made against desire and pleasure, thereby opening the doors permanently to suspicion, it is love itself that is attacked. It is therefore not too much to ask that the lords and masters we have given ourselves should be summoned before the court. The scandal is not to be found in the grotesque exchanges which Panizza has put in their mouths; it is to be found wholly in the verdict that we have intended or allowed them to pronounce.

Under the ruins heaped upon him, a plant continues to grow, whose roots, we feel certain, remain sound; it is nothing more than *sympathie.* It is this *sympathie* which provides the profound human motivation of the play, and it centers irresistibly around the Devil. This is so because he alone, of all the play's imaginary characters, remains enterprising and effective. Even when he contrives the most frightful trap for us—on orders—we are so constituted that we cannot help being fascinated by his thought, as if it were our own dipped in mercury. Also, since his meanderings are copied after our own, we are touched by his tale of woe and by his plaints, minimal as they are, because of his undeniable *competence.* Never has the Devil appeared closer to us than as we watch him overcome, with all the skill of his intelligence, an Olympus that is so down-at-the-heel. He forces us to recognize his mastery in matters of logic and strategy. The tradition which depicts him as condemned to carrying out the menial tasks of the Creator shows him here as eminently up to his job. But there is more: he succeeds in moving us even by his inadequacies and his weaknesses, as when he dreams of being in the Gotha, whereas the exploit which we watch him accomplish would suffice to anoint him Prince of Guile and Archon of the entire world.

In Panizza the Eternal Feminine retains all of its allure, even though its attraction does not operate, as it does in Goethe, in an upward direction. From Mary to the various creatures whom, one after the other, the Devil calls forth from the Field of the Dead, all of them—with the moving exception of Héloïse—vie with one another in their obtuseness and suggest disaster. This is the secret of the enduring attraction which they exercise and which gives the measure of the ravages they have caused. Among such as these the Devil can never be too difficult as to the choice of his partner—the one whose beauty must contain the most gratuitous perversion—in order to bring about within the limits prescribed his masterpiece of perdition: the Woman, lethally seductive down unto the depths of her flesh while she makes party to her sumptuous unconcern, as if lacking in some essential quality of self, all the glories of the night.

THE COUNCIL OF LOVE

CHARACTERS

GOD THE FATHER

JESUS CHRIST

THE VIRGIN MARY

THE DEVIL

THE WOMAN

A CHERUB

FIRST ANGEL

SECOND ANGEL

THIRD ANGEL

Figures from Hell

HELEN OF TROY

PHRYNE

HÉLOÏSE

AGRIPPINA

SALOME

RODRIGO BORGIA, POPE ALEXANDER VI

Children of the Pope

GIROLAMA BORGIA, *wife of Cesarini (mother unknown)*

ISABELLA BORGIA, *wife of Matuzzi (mother unknown)*

PIER LUIGI BORGIA *(by Vanozza), Duke of Gandia*

DON GIOVANNI BORGIA, *Count of Celano (by Vanozza)*

CESARE BORGIA, *Duke of Romagna (by Vanozza)*

DON GIOFFRE BORGIA, *Count of Cariati (by Vanozza)*

3

DONNA LUCREZIA BORGIA, *Duchess of Bisaglie (by Vanozza)*

LAURA BORGIA, *not yet of age (by Julia Farnese, wife of Orsini)*

GIOVANNI BORGIA, *not yet of age (by Julia Farnese, wife of Orsini)*

Mistresses of the Pope

VANOZZA

JULIA FARNESE, *wife of Orsini*

ALESSANDRO FARNESE, *her brother, Cardinal*

DONNA SANCIA, *daughter-in-law of the Pope, wife of Don Gioffre*

ADRIANA MILA, *confidante of the Pope, governess to his children*

Nephews of the Pope

FRANCESCO BORGIA, *Archbishop of Cosenza, Treasurer of the Pope*

LUIGI PIETRO BORGIA, *Cardinal-Deacon of Santa Maria*

COLLERANDO BORGIA, *Bishop of Coria and Monreale*

RODRIGO BORGIA, *Captain of the Pope's Guard*

Confidants of the Pope

GIOVANNI LOPEZ, *Bishop of Perugia*

PIETRO CARANZA, *Privy Councilor*

JUAN MARADES, *Bishop of Toul, Private Steward*

GIOVANNI VERA DA ERCILLA, *Member of the College of Cardinals*

REMOLINA DA ILERDA, *Member of the College of Cardinals*

BURCARD, *Master of Ceremonies to the Pope*

A PRIEST

FIRST NOBLEMAN

SECOND NOBLEMAN

THIRD NOBLEMAN

Actors

       PULCINELLO
       COLOMBINA

       A COURTESAN

       THE HOLY GHOST, ARCHANGELS, OLD AND YOUNG
       ANGELS, CUPIDS, MARY MAGDALENE, APOSTLES,
       MARTYRS, SISTERS OF CHARITY, A MESSENGER,
       ANIMALS, BUFFOONS, GHOSTS, CHURCH DIGNITARIES,
       OFFICIALS OF THE POPE'S COURT, PAPAL NUNCIOS,
       ROMAN LADIES, COURTIERS, COURTESANS, ACTORS,
       SINGERS, WRESTLERS, SOLDIERS, COMMON PEOPLE.

Time:

       *Spring 1495, date of the first outbreak of syphilis
       recorded in history.*

Act One

$\mathfrak{S}$CENE 1

*Heaven. A Throne Room. Three Angels dressed in
swan-white down. They wear tight-fitting knee pants with
knee hose. They have little wings like Cupids', and short
powdered hair. White satin shoes. They are holding feather
dusters in their hands.*

FIRST ANGEL:
> He's sleeping late again today.

SECOND ANGEL:
> So don't complain! Would you rather hear him
> cough and spit and curse? Maybe you'd like to
> watch him sit and drool and stare into empty space
> from morning till night. No one ever gets any peace
> around here any more.

THIRD ANGEL:
> Yes, I've noticed that up here!

FIRST ANGEL:
> Say, did we fix the throne?

SECOND ANGEL:
> My God, you're right! We've got to brace the
> throne. It wobbled yesterday.

THIRD ANGEL:
> Who wobbled yesterday?

FIRST ANGEL:
> The throne, you ass!

THIRD ANGEL (*amazed*):

> The throne? Why should the throne wobble?

FIRST ANGEL:

> Well, it did.

THIRD ANGEL:

> It did? But how can anything wobble up here?

FIRST AND SECOND ANGELS (*bursting out laughing*):

> Ha! Ha! Ha!

THIRD ANGEL (*more and more serious and surprised*):

> Yes, how can the Holy Throne wobble?

FIRST ANGEL (*speaking sharply*):

> You stupid fool! Because just about everything is falling apart up here! Gods, furniture, the fringe, the wallpaper.

THIRD ANGEL (*trembling from within*):

> Oh, God, if Mother only knew.

SECOND ANGEL (*frowning and sneering*):

> Your mother? What's your mother got to do with it, silly?

THIRD ANGEL:

> Today she had her sixtieth mass said for the peace of my soul.

FIRST AND SECOND ANGELS (*with increasing surprise*):

> For the peace of your soul? (*Both burst out laughing.*) Say, just how old are you, anyway?

THIRD ANGEL (*thinking for a moment and then quoting solemnly*):

> "In the eyes of God a thousand years are as but a single day. A single day is as a thousand years."

FIRST AND SECOND ANGELS (*stopping her and bringing her back to the subject*):
> Yes, yes, yes! That's fine! We know all that! But how old were you down there?

THIRD ANGEL (*childlike*):
> Just fourteen!

FIRST ANGEL (*laughing*):
> And so you need masses said for the peace of your soul?

THIRD ANGEL (*timidly*):
> You mean you don't know that I'm dead?

FIRST AND SECOND ANGELS (*laughing still louder*):
> Ha, ha, ha, ha! Hee, hee, hee! Of course we do. Otherwise you wouldn't be here!

THIRD ANGEL (*with imperturbable seriousness*):
> But what you don't know is that I died in a state of mortal sin!

FIRST AND SECOND ANGELS (*laughing again*):
> Mortal sin yet! You poor thing! So what did you do?

The Third Angel, at a loss for words, stares at her companions and folds her hands.

SECOND ANGEL (*mocking*):
> You mean you didn't study your lessons? You spilled ink on your homework?

THIRD ANGEL (*with tense anguish*):
> Oh, I'm so afraid! Promise you won't tell anyone!

FIRST AND SECOND ANGELS (*shaking with laughter*):
> What? Not tell anyone? Up here?

THIRD ANGEL (*surprised*):
> You mean you already know?

FIRST ANGEL:
> No! But go ahead. We'll find out anyway!

SECOND ANGEL:
> Come on, don't be afraid! What happened?

THIRD ANGEL:
> Oh . . . a great big man crushed me to death!

FIRST ANGEL (*accenting the individual words*):
> Crushed . . . you . . . to death?

THIRD ANGEL:
> Maybe it was poison.

SECOND ANGEL (*same as before*):
> Poi . . . son!

THIRD ANGEL (*naïvely*):
> I can't remember what Mother said.

FIRST ANGEL (*with increasing astonishment*):
> You mean your mother was there?

THIRD ANGEL (*telling the story with shining eyes*):
> She was in the next room, but the door was half open. Then a tall old man walked in. Mother said to let him go ahead, that he was the director of the school and that he was very strict, that if I did whatever I was told, I would get good grades. The tall old man . . .

FIRST AND SECOND ANGELS (*urging her on*):
> Yes, yes . . . the tall old man? . . .

THIRD ANGEL (*continuing*):
> . . . was very strong.

FIRST AND SECOND ANGELS (*looking at each other and imitating the Third Angel*):

> The tall old man was very strong!

SECOND ANGEL:

> It sounds like a schoolbook.

FIRST ANGEL (*shaking the Third Angel*):

> So tell us what the tall old man did!

THIRD ANGEL (*bursting out with it*):

> He crushed me and poisoned me and spewed his hot breath into my face and wanted to get inside of me. . . .

FIRST AND SECOND ANGELS (*clasping their hands and pretending to be horrified*):

> What? And your mother didn't come to your rescue?

THIRD ANGEL:

> She was looking through the crack in the door and kept saying over and over, "Be a good girl, Lili, be a good girl."

SECOND ANGEL:

> And then what?

THIRD ANGEL:

> Then I just lay on the bed . . . sobbing.

FIRST ANGEL:

> And then what?

THIRD ANGEL (*trying to remember*):

> . . . I heard Mother talking with the man.

SECOND ANGEL:

> What were they saying?

THIRD ANGEL (*trying hard to remember*):

   . . . I can't remember. . . . They were in the next room. . . . I heard someone say five hundred. . . .

FIRST ANGEL:

   Then what?

THIRD ANGEL (*taking more and more time to remember*):

   . . . Mother came into the room. . . . She said that now we had lots of money and that we could live happily for the rest of our days. . . . (*She forgets the rest.*)

FIRST ANGEL (*insistently*):

   Then what?

SECOND ANGEL (*also insistently*):

   Then what? Then what?

THIRD ANGEL (*almost radiant, inspired*):

   Then . . . I died.

The First and Second Angels step apart, clasp their hands over their heads, and give long shrill screams, like overexcited little girls releasing some pent-up emotion. Then they begin running in wide circles around the room, spinning and humming like tops. The Third Angel continues to stand transfixed.

FIRST ANGEL (*out of breath from so much activity*):

   Sixty thousand masses for the peace of your soul!

THIRD ANGEL (*whimpering and afraid*):

   I died in a state of mortal sin!

SECOND ANGEL (*moral and severe*):

   And so that's the money your mother pays for the masses with!

THIRD ANGEL (*naïve and failing to understand*):
Oh, Mother only used a part of the money.

TWO OLDER ANGELS (*burst in shouting*):
He's coming!—*He*'s coming!—Is everything ready?

The three angels separate and set to work.

FIRST ANGEL:
For God's sake, be sure the throne is steady!

One of the angels attends to the throne. Meanwhile other angels arrive, bringing blankets, pillows, cushions, and so on.

SECOND ANGEL (*hops onto the throne and checks it all over*):
All set!

FIRST ANGEL (*to the Third Angel, who is still too timid to help and watches the whole business with curiosity*):
You'll tell us the rest later on. Right now you stick with us!

The Two Older Angels, who have been standing guard at the door, now rush back, waving their arms and shouting again.

TWO OLDER ANGELS:
He's coming! *He*'s coming!

Offstage one can hear a dragging, scraping kind of noise.

$\mathfrak{S}$CENE 2

*The same characters as before. God the Father enters. He is
a very old man with silver-white hair and beard. Heavy bags
under bright blue, staring eyes. His head is bent. He has a
backward curvature of the spine. He is wearing a long
dirty-white robe. He is supported on both sides by two
Cherubim. He coughs. His throat rattles. He gropes His
way awkwardly, leaning forward, dragging His feet. Two
angels stand one on each side of the throne and support it.
The others fall to their knees, bow their heads to the ground,
and extend their arms.*

    *Following God the Father, an endless procession of
Angels, Seraphim, Guards, Attendants. All are female or
sexless. Their faces express boredom, impertinence, worry,
anxiety. Also a number of Sisters of Charity, dressed like
nuns, carrying medicine bottles, blankets, spittoons, etc.
Slowly and carefully they accompany God the Father to the
throne. They help Him up the two steps, take hold of His
legs from below and lift them. They then turn Him around
and help Him to sit down slowly on the seat, which is of
ancient Byzantine style, richly decorated with mosaics.
Meanwhile two angels in front of God the Father, two
behind, and one on each side support Him or let Him lean on
them. Another angel brings crutches.*

GOD THE FATHER (*sinking down onto the throne, uttering a desperate,
long, weary, hoarse sigh*):
Ah!

> *He stares motionless into space, breathing hard. All the*
> *angels, including those who until now have remained*
> *kneeling, begin to run about in a frenzy of activity.*

CHERUB (*whispering in a tone of urgent command*):
>   The footstool!

AN ANGEL (*executing the command in haste*):
>   The footstool!

CHERUB (*propping His legs with the footstool and speaking as*
>   *above*):
>   The hot-water bottle!

AN ANGEL (*bringing it*):
>   The hot-water bottle!

CHERUB (*as above*):
>   The foot-warmer!

AN ANGEL (*hurrying*):
>   The foot-warmer!

CHERUB (*as above*):
>   The lap robe!

AN ANGEL (*bringing it, hurrying*):
>   The lap robe!

CHERUB (*in a tone of urgent command*):
>   The pillow!

AN ANGEL (*bringing it*):
>   The pillow!

CHERUB (*as above*):
>   The shawl!

AN ANGEL:
>   The shawl!

CHERUB (*more and more urgently*):
> The armrests!

AN ANGEL (*bringing two pads for the arms of the throne*):
> The armrests!

CHERUB (*as above*):
> The scarf!

AN ANGEL (*bringing a bright red silk cloth*):
> The scarf!

> *While the Cherub wraps the scarf around the old man's neck, one hears God the Father moaning and groaning in a hoarse, inarticulate voice.*

GOD THE FATHER:
> Uh!—Uh!—Uh!

SEVERAL ANGELS:
> What's the matter! What's wrong? Help! Help! What's the matter with Him?

GOD THE FATHER (*with bowed head, continuing to groan*):
> Uh!—Uh!—Uh!

ALL ANGELS (*gathering in great confusion around the throne, some kneeling and observing God the Father with intense anguish*):
> Help! Help! What's the matter? What's the matter? Holy Majesty, what's the matter? He's dying in front of our eyes! Call Mary! Call the Man! Help! Help!

GOD THE FATHER (*continues to moan; heavy tears stream from His eyes because of the effort He makes*):
> Uh!—Uh! (*Sounds of clearing His throat, hawking, gagging and spitting.*)

AN ANGEL (*jumping up triumphantly, speaking in a loud, clear voice*):
> The spitting cup!

ALL ANGELS (*jumping up, speaking in dissonant soprano voices and with relief*):
> The spitting cup!

> *They go quickly to a table where medicine bottles, wine bottles, cookie jars, etc., are standing, and return with a rose-colored crystal goblet.*
>
> *God the Father clears His throat noisily and with great effort finally relieves Himself. An angel removes the spitting cup. Accompanied by others, he carries it solemnly offstage. Another angel wipes the old man's beard with a silk cloth. Then all assemble, expectantly, in a crowd around God the Father. The latter first stares glassily into space for a while, turning His head in a circle; then suddenly He seizes His crutches with trembling hands and, thrusting out unexpectedly as He gives a hoarse, menacing pretense of a roar, stabs at the angels.*

GOD THE FATHER:
> Woo! Woo!

> *With shrill screams the angels scatter and take flight. A single cherub remains. Hiding his face in his hands, he sinks to his knees before God the Father. There is a long pause.*

Scene 3

God the Father. The Cherub. The latter is a sexless angel with white wings and a beautiful face. He resembles Antinous. He remains kneeling during the entire scene.

GOD THE FATHER (*after looking down at him for a long while, speaking very calmly and in a deep baritone*):
Does the earth still turn in its orbit?

CHERUB (*looking up, solemnly*):
The earth turns in its orbit!

Pause.

GOD THE FATHER (*as before*):
Has the sun already risen?

CHERUB (*hesitating*):
The sun hangs motionless, most Holy Father!

GOD THE FATHER (*calm, indifferent*):
The sun hangs motionless? Ah, yes, I forgot. I can hardly see it any more.

CHERUB:
Do your eyes still hurt, Sacred Father?

GOD THE FATHER:
Bad! They're bad! God, but I've gotten old!

CHERUB (*solemnly*):
To you a thousand years are as but a single day!

GOD THE FATHER:

> Yes, yes! But even so they pass!

CHERUB:

> You'll be well again, Ancient Holy One.

GOD THE FATHER:

> No, I'll never be well again! (*In an outburst*) God, but it's ghastly to be so old! My God, it's horrible to go on living in eternal decrepitude! Monstrous to be a God that's gone blind!

CHERUB:

> Your sight will come back, most Divine, most Holy Father!

GOD THE FATHER (*with conviction*):

> No, it won't! I'll never see again! I'll just go on getting older and older . . . sicker and sicker . . . weaker and weaker! God, if only I could die!

CHERUB (*gently*):

> You won't die! You can't die! You mustn't die!

GOD THE FATHER (*moved, weeping softly*):

> Oh, my poor legs! They're twisted, swollen, full of water, cramped, decayed . . . (*rubs His knees*).

The Cherub slides close to God the Father, lays his head on one of His knees, and strokes the other with his hand. In soft lament and with deep compassion, he does a childish imitation of the old man.

CHERUB:

> Oh, your poor legs! They're twisted, swollen, full of water, cramped, decayed . . . oh, oh!

GOD THE FATHER (*weeping bitterly*):

> My feet are full of gout . . . the bones are all gone
> . . . they burn with pain and twitch and
> throb. . . .

CHERUB (*sliding down to the old man's feet, caressing them and moaning*):

> Your feet are full of gout . . . the bones are all
> gone . . . they burn with pain and twitch and throb
> . . . oh, oh!

GOD THE FATHER (*breaking into heavy sobs of pain*):

> Oh, oh!

CHERUB (*throwing himself to the floor, embracing both of God's feet, laying a cheek against them and sobbing*):

> Oh, God . . . God . . . God! . . .

God the Father is very moved. He tries to bend down, extending both arms toward the child, but can't reach him. Heavy tears fall on the Cherub's head. The Cherub, aware of what is happening, rises quickly and in a half-kneeling position comes close to the old man. He puts his arms around Him. God the Father passionately seizes the head of the child with both hands, presses His tear-stained face against the child's cheeks, and, sobbing, ardently kisses his brow, eyes, and hair. Both, seeking release in tears, continue to embrace each other without speaking until the violent outburst of the old man begins to abate. At this point there is a knock at the door.

CHERUB (*starting up*):

> There's someone at the door!

GOD THE FATHER (*tired*):

> See who it is!

CHERUB (*returning after a whispered conversation at the door*):
It's a messenger. He has news for You. He says it's
very urgent.

GOD THE FATHER (*indifferent*):
Tell him to come in.

$\mathfrak{S}$CENE 4

The same characters as before. The Messenger has wings both at his shoulders and at his feet. He is of mature age. He is accompanied by two other angels. They enter in a state of great agitation.

MESSENGER (*sinking to the ground and kissing the floor, then rising to a kneeling position*):

My Lord, I come from Italy, from Naples. I have horrible things to report to you. The stench from the cesspools of sin can be smelled even in Heaven! The bonds of all morality are loosed! Our Holy Commandments, given by You on Sinai, are turned to derision! The city, besieged by the French, indulges in the most horrifying abominations! Women bare their breasts and run through the streets like shameless, lascivious beasts! The men burn like he-goats! Vice is rampant! The sea waves lash into their streets! The sun hides its face! And yet they will heed no sign of Heaven or of Earth. All barriers of social class are let down! The King breaks into the brothel while the lackey invades the palace to get at the King's hired whores! Dogs and roosters have their seasons, but in Naples men are animals the whole year long! The entire city is a boiling kettle of lust! There is more love-madness in Italy than in any other place in Europe, but Naples is to Italy what Italy is to the rest of the world! The

siege has raised the delirium of the sexes to such a
pitch that there is no longer any mercy for old age
or pity for youth! Genitals of huge proportions are
paraded on holidays like divinities through the
streets, accompanied by rows of dancing maidens
and worshiped like all-powerful idols! In your
Church I have seen a priest before the altar with a
prostitute. . . .

*God the Father has listened to the whole story with
increasing dismay. Now He gets up from His throne with a
supreme effort and extends His clenched fist.*

GOD THE FATHER:
    I will smash them to bits!

All fall to the floor and hide their faces.

CHERUB (*in a pleading manner*):
    Don't, don't, beloved Holy Father! If you do, you
    will have no men left!

GOD THE FATHER (*staring long at the Cherub with open mouth,
    reflecting*):
    Yes, yes, you're right. I forgot. (*Sinking back on His
    throne*) The time for creation is past. I am too old.
    And My children are not able.

CHERUB (*naïvely*):
    Be at peace, Ancient Holy One! You will show
    Your awesome face among the clouds. You will
    speak Your wrath to the Neapolitans, and they will
    tremble.

GOD THE FATHER:
    They won't tremble! They'll laugh at Me! They
    know that all I can do is talk. They know that down

there they're on their own ground, free to court and love and hate as they please! They don't need Me! (*Starting up, to the Messenger*): You, go get My daughter, the Blessed Virgin! And go get My Son! And tell My cherubim and My Angels of Death to hold themselves ready for My Holy command! And go tell the Devil that he should report to Me! We shall hold a Council and We shall see what is to be done about this loathsome thing!

The Messenger, angels, and cherubim leave noisily. Only the beautiful Cherub remains. He fusses over the exhausted old man, assists Him back onto His throne, arranges the footstool and hot-water bottle, ties the scarf around His neck, wipes His face and beard, and at last snuggles down at His feet. Meanwhile the old man takes one of the Cherub's hands and holds it in His own. Mute scene.

$\mathbf{S}$CENE 5

The same characters as before. Mary enters through the main door. She is accompanied by a crowd of young Angels dressed like cupids, as well as full-grown Boy Angels carrying long-stemmed lilies. The young angels rush ahead of Mary and strew flowers in her path. Mary's bearing is proud and haughty. She wears a small crown and is dressed in star-covered blue. The white silk of an undergarment shows through the front of her gown. She makes a stiff, courtly bow before the throne of God the Father where the Cherub is no longer on the steps. She then goes to a second throne, which has meanwhile been made ready by servant-angels; it stands somewhat apart from God the Father's, but also against the wall. Its tall back and style make it seem to belong to the period of the troubadours.

Mary remains there during the following scene, surrounded by her body of angels and busying herself exclusively with her appearance. She looks at herself in a small mirror and sprays herself with sweet-smelling perfumes. The soft whispering of mischievous, flirtatious cupids can be heard around her throne. Meanwhile, on the opposite side, to the left of the stage and toward the front, the three angels from the first scene are conversing.

FIRST ANGEL:
The Man is coming.

SECOND ANGEL (*clapping his hands*):
The Man, the Man is coming.

THIRD ANGEL (*listening seriously*):
> The Man? Who is the Man?

SECOND ANGEL:
> The Man, you little monkey, the Man is the Man.

FIRST ANGEL (*like a teacher*):
> The most beautiful, the most tender, the sweetest Man, the only Man . . . in all of Heaven. That's who the Man is!

THIRD ANGEL (*curious*):
> Is he young?

FIRST ANGEL:
> Like a new palm tree.

THIRD ANGEL (*after a moment of thought*):
> Is he younger than that old man over there?

FIRST AND SECOND ANGELS (*together*):
> A hundred thousand times younger!

THIRD ANGEL (*thinking further*):
> Is he younger than that beautiful lady over there?

FIRST AND SECOND ANGELS:
> A thousand times, a thousand times younger!

THIRD ANGEL (*still reflecting*):
> Is he younger than that nasty old man down on earth?

FIRST AND SECOND ANGELS (*as above*):
> Infinitely, infinitely younger!

THIRD ANGEL (*becoming interested*):
> Is he beautiful?

SECOND ANGEL:
> Like white ivory!

THIRD ANGEL:
>Is he slender?

FIRST ANGEL:
>Like a fir tree!

THIRD ANGEL:
>What are his eyes like?

SECOND ANGEL:
>Like a gazelle's.

THIRD ANGEL:
>How does he speak?

FIRST ANGEL (*thoughtful*):
>Like an aeolian harp! But sad, sad!

THIRD ANGEL (*with pity*):
>Why is the Man sad?

SECOND ANGEL:
>Because they hurt Him.

The Third Angel is wide-eyed, in silent amazement.

FIRST ANGEL:
>They pierced His hands!

SECOND ANGEL:
>They pierced His feet!

FIRST ANGEL:
>They pierced His side!

SECOND ANGEL:
>You can see drops of blood on His brow underneath His hair.

THIRD ANGEL (*listening with growing wonder*):
>But He's alive?

FIRST AND SECOND ANGELS:
He's alive!

Offstage one can hear a procession approach. A crowd of young, girlish Angels rush in.

FIRST AND SECOND ANGELS:
The Man is coming!

THIRD ANGEL (*repeating softly*):
The Man is coming.

The angels step back in order to make room.

THE GIRLISH ANGELS (*twittering and tittering*):
The Man! The Man!

Christ, with outstretched arms crossed in front (Ecce Homo position), enters in a white robe over which He wears a purple cloak. He comes as King of the Jews, walking with a halting step. His head is bowed, and His expression is infinitely sad. He is surrounded by angels, mostly of mature age, who carry the Cross and instruments of His martyrdom. In His retinue are Apostles, Martyrs, Mary Magdalene, Mourning Women. He is very youthful and pale. He has dark hair and a soft, downy beard. He is tall and His appearance is ethereal. Even His followers seem to be in a state of weakness and deep dejection. The younger angels press around Him with eyes afire, trying to touch the hem of His robe. While God the Father watches Him with indifference, He proceeds, completely unnoticed by Mary, lost in His passivity and paying attention to no one, toward a throne which has meanwhile been set up for Him a little to one side of the others. It has the primitive shape of a Jewish

*lectern. There, still maintaining His Ecce Homo position,
He sits down in complete apathy while His followers gather
around Him.*

*After all are assembled and the groups of angels have
kneeled in front of the three thrones where they occupy the
entire front portion of the stage:*

GOD THE FATHER (*solemnly and with great feeling*):
Are we all assembled?

(*At this moment a flash of fire streaks, whistling like a
rocket, straight across the domed ceiling of the room. The
sound of its clash sinks away into the distance: It is the Holy
Ghost. All look upward in an attitude of solemnity. The
angels stand with outstretched arms. Only Mary, leaning her
head passively against the left arm of the throne, stares
indifferently into space. Christ crosses His arms over His
chest, bows His head even more, and remains for a long
while in an attitude of deep contrition.*)

(*After a pause during which all return to their previous
positions*) We have called you together here to take
counsel with you in a difficult and horrible matter.
In total contempt of my commandments, mankind
is indulging in the worship of idols, self-destruction,
the most horrible debauchery, the most heinous
abominations. In a city . . . in Asia . . . in . . . in
. . . where is that city anyway?

CHERUB (*standing nearest to God the Father and raising clasped
hands*):
In Naples, most Holy Father.

GOD THE FATHER (*remembering*):
Yes! In Naples . . . they have torn off their
clothing, which was intended as a protection to

natural modesty, and now they mingle like animals with ruthless scorn for the limits and restrictions set to the desires of the flesh! Therefore, Our Heavenly Wrath . . .

MARY (*breaking in, frivolously*):
Oh, yes, I've heard of that.

GOD THE FATHER (*looking up with surprise*):
What? What's that?

MARY (*as above*):
Yes, I know all about it. The messenger came to see me first . . . (*She claps her hand suddenly to her mouth as if to recall her words.*)

God the Father, pale with rage, attempts to continue, looks around to find the Messenger in the crowd, then glances back toward Mary and snorts with anger. With eloquent eyes the Cherub silently implores the old man to control Himself.

GOD THE FATHER (*swallowing His rage and speaking bitterly*):
I see that you are all aware of the situation. (*He continues to struggle for a moment with His anger.*)
On Our own Authority, We have decided that the most terrible punishment . . .

MARY (*interrupting*):
You can't make a purse out of a sow's ear.

CHRIST (*looking up with dull, glassy eyes and repeating thickly in the hollow voice of a consumptive*):
No, you can't make a purse out of a sow's ear.

ANGELS (*to each other, nudging each other*):
The Man! The Man!

MARY MAGDALENE (*bitterly*):
> But what have they done?

MARY (*speaking sharply*):
> I'll tell you later! They're just filthy, that's all.

GOD THE FATHER (*furious*):
> We shall wipe them out!

CHRIST (*as above*):
> Yes, yes, we shall wipe them out!

CHORUS OF APOSTLES, MARTYRS, ANGELS (*lamenting*):
> Oh! Oh! Oh!

CHRIST (*not understanding*):
> Huh?

MARY (*speaking sharply and with authority*):
> Not at all! That won't do! We've got to have them!

CHRIST (*repeating Mary's words*):
> Yes, yes, we've got to have them.

GOD THE FATHER (*finding Himself in the minority, angrily*):
> We've got to have them? Well, I intend to rub them
> out, filthy creatures. I intend, I intend to have a
> nice clean Earth again . . . with animals in the
> forests . . .

MARY (*caustic*):
> Well, if we are to have animals, we must have men.

MARY MAGDALENE (*compassionately*):
> Sin can purify.

GOD THE FATHER:
> They gorge themselves on sin as if they were eating
> cake! Until they burst! Until they rot!

MARY (*with a sharpness in her voice*):

> In the final analysis you've got to allow them sex.
> You can't refuse them a little taste of lust! Other-
> wise they'll go hang themselves on the first tree!

> (*The Old Man watches her more and more angrily; sparks
> are about to fly.*)

> Oh, at night! At night! Or in the spring! At certain
> times of the year! When the moon is out! . . .
> Measure! . . . Measure! . . . Purpose!

GOD THE FATHER (*with increasing anger*):

> I'll cut them down like a pair of lascivious dogs!
> Right at the height of their pleasure!

> *A movement in the crowd. The younger angels look at each
> other in dismay.*

MARY (*with the same sharpness*):

> And who will create mankind then?

> *While the Apostles consult with each other in concern and a
> painful uneasiness fills the room, the Old Man, breathing
> hard, stares into space with glowing eyes. His expression
> grows darker and darker. A rasping, rattling sound comes
> from His throat. He seems to be on the verge of an attack. He
> waves His arms, throws blankets and crutches from Him,
> groans and roars. They run to help Him, bringing spitting
> cup and smelling bottles. Mary springs to her feet in concern.
> Christ, too weak to stand, looks on with brooding, glassy
> eyes. There is great confusion. With wild gestures the Old
> Man refuses all help and support, gathers His strength, and
> roars with terrifying effort.*

GOD THE FATHER:

> I will strike them down! I'll grind them into the dust! I'll pound them to pulp in the mortar of my wrath!
>
> *He is about to get up and is preparing to strike an irreparable blow that will be an irreparable act of omnipotence.*

CHERUB (*springing forward at this moment, throwing himself before the Old Man, and in an imploring voice*):

> Most Holy, most Godly Father, tomorrow is Easter! On earth they are eating the Paschal Meal!

CHORUS OF APOSTLES, MARTYRS, OLDER ANGELS (*chiming in*):

> They are eating the Paschal Meal!

GOD THE FATHER (*brought up short*):

> What are they eating?

CHERUB AND OTHERS:

> They are eating the Paschal Meal!

GOD THE FATHER (*looking around in astonishment*):

> They're eating the Paschal Meal?

CHORUS OF APOSTLES:

> They're eating the Easter Lamb!

CHERUB:

> They're celebrating the Last Supper!

GOD THE FATHER (*reflecting*):

> The Last Supper?

CHERUB:

> They're eating the flesh and blood of Christ!

GOD THE FATHER (*with a touch of feeling*):

> My Son, they're eating You!

CHRIST (*in a dull voice*):
> Yes, they're eating Me.

MARY (*with a pretense of tenderness*):
> My beloved Son, Whom I carried in my womb!

CHRIST (*childlike*):
> Whom you carried in your womb.

GOD THE FATHER (*mechanically*):
> Whom she carried in her womb.

THE YOUNGER ANGELS (*whispering among themselves*):
> The Man! The Man!

MARY (*as above*):
> They're eating You!

CHRIST (*as above*):
> They're eating Me.

GOD THE FATHER (*as above*):
> They're eating Him.

CHRIST (*starting up*):
> Yes, and meanwhile up here We get weaker and weaker, sicker and sicker! It's horrible! (*Coughs.*) Down there they eat Me and become healthy and free of sin, while here, day after day, We waste away. Down there they gorge themselves on sin until they burst! Then they partake of Me and thrive and are free of sin and get thick and fat! And We get sick and thin. Ah, this damnable game We play! Once, just once, I'd like to turn the tables on them and eat Myself sick and let them starve! (*He breaks into a consumptive cough.*)

MARY (*springing up and hurrying to him, worried*):
> My God, my Son, don't forget that You're invulner-

able. . . . You're a God. . . . You're inedible. (*She draws His head to her breast and caresses Him.*)

Christ sobs deeply on Mary's breast.

THE YOUNGER ANGELS (*whispering among themselves*):
  The Man! The Man!

GOD THE FATHER (*after a pause, much calmer, to the Cherub*):
  Just who all are celebrating Easter down there?

CHERUB (*responding promptly*):
  The Christians, Holy Father. Your believers, Divine Master! Your children who place their hope in You! The good people, the Catholics, Your one and only Holy Church, Your priests, the Bishops, the Pope!

GOD THE FATHER (*pleased, genially*):
  You mean that? Well, so let's have a look!

MARY (*delighted that a solution has been found*): Yes, let's have a look! (*To Christ*):
  Come, my Son, we must watch this. It will relax You!

  There is great general relief. The tight groups spread out. The younger angels leave the room. Servant-angels busy themselves with the thrones, bringing everything back into splendid, trim order. The medical equipment is taken away and replaced by strange, large tripods brought in during the following scene. The groups of Apostles, Martyrs, Angels, Sisters of Charity withdraw in solemn order so that, at last, only the three divinities, the Cherub, and a few older angels remain.

GOD THE FATHER (*settling comfortably in a half-reclining position on His throne and speaking in a deep, sonorous, solemn voice*): Let the incense and the incense burners be brought in! And let omniscience and omnipresence be made manifest in Us.

The tripods are placed in the middle of the room. A brown incense mixed with sandalwood is placed in them and lighted. The doors are closed. The servant-angels withdraw and finally the Cherub. Amid the spreading clouds of steam one can see the three divinities slowly lean back and close their eyes.

THE CURTAIN FALLS

Act Two

*A stately hall in the Pope's palace in Rome. At the back of
the stage the hall ends in a series of arcades surmounted by a
gallery with rounded arches. Beyond the back wall of the
hall lies the private chapel of the Pope, with which there is
communication through windows on the upper gallery. The
latter is consequently at about the same level as the choir of
the chapel.*

*The entire left side of the stage (as seen from the stage) is
taken up by the Pope, his family, the Papal court, and the
banqueting guests. The tables are richly decked with costly
silver and bright, impressively tall, three-branched
candelabra.*

*The entire middle and right side, with the exception of a
few groups forming and conversing on the extreme right,
remain free for the action and masquerades that will follow.*

*It is toward evening on the first day of Easter 1495. The
tables are being cleared. The Pope wears the comfortable,
unassuming dress of a house-prelate (violet with velvet trim)
and a small, round velvet cap. The others are all richly
dressed. Even the servants are dazzling. There is constant
movement. Lively conversation. Frequent peals of laughter.
There are musicians in the background under the arches. The
gallery is filled with spectators from among the common*

This act is based on an account given in Burcardi, Master of
Ceremonies to Alexander VI, *Diarium*, ed. Thuasne (Paris,
1885).

*people. In the hall groups form, exchange news, then break
up.*

*In addition to the Pope (Rodrigo Borgia, Alexander VI),
a man in his sixties, there are his nine children: Girolama,
Isabella, Pier Luigi, Don Giovanni (Count of Celano),
Cesare, Don Gioffre, Lucrezia, fifteen years old, blond, gay,
and childlike; Laura, and Don Giovanni Borgia, a boy. Also
his daughters-in-law and sons-in-law, among them Donna
Sancia, the wife of Don Gioffre; his nephews and relatives,
among them Collerando Borgia, Almoner, Bishop of Coria
and Monreale; Francesco Borgia, Archbishop of Cosenza,
Treasurer of the Pope; Luigi Pietro Borgia,
Cardinal-Deacon of Santa Maria; Rodrigo Borgia, Captain
of the Pope's Guard; his confidants, among them Giovanni
Lopez, Bishop of Perugia; Pietro Caranza, Privy Councilor;
Giovanni Vera da Ercilla and Remolina da Ilerda, Members
of the College of Cardinals; Juan Marades, Bishop of Toul,
Private Steward; The Two Mistresses of the Pope: his
former mistress, Vanozza, now fifty-three; and his present
mistress, Julia Farnese, twenty-one. The latter is with her
husband, Orsini, and her brother, Cardinal Alessandro
Farnese; the Pope's confidante, Adriana Mila, governess to
his children; Burcard, Master of Ceremonies to the Pope.
Archbishops, Bishops, Cardinals, Papal Dignitaries,
Roman Ladies, Soldiers and Servants, Common People.
Later Courtesans and Actors.*

DON GIOFFRE:

What a boring sermon that Spaniard gave again
today!

THE POPE:

Atrocious! You just can't listen to him.

DONNA SANCIA (*to Lucrezia*):

I kept waving at you, but you didn't understand.

LUCREZIA (*sleepily*):

That's because Pietro kept kicking me as usual.

DON GIOFFRE:

His Holiness didn't manage a great deal better!
The Spaniard went right on preaching even though
His Holiness gave unmistakable signs of displeas-
ure.

THE POPE:

He comes from Valencia where they're as stubborn
as goats. Just let one of them get started and he'll
never stop! The slightest emotion becomes a rocket!
They don't just talk, they club you over the head!

Bursts of laughter.

FRANCESCO BORGIA:

But he did make an honest try.

THE POPE:

Honesty can be extremely awkward!

DON GIOFFRE:

Yes, but the people were eating out of his hand.
They were insane, possessed! You'd have thought
they'd seen a ghost, the way they stared!

DON GIOVANNI:

That was because Donna Sancia kept whispering
and giggling.

DONNA SANCIA:

No, it was because Lucrezia kept eating candy.

LUCREZIA:

No, it was because Laura was snoozing and snor-
ing!

DON GIOFFRE:

I think it was because they couldn't take their eyes off the pearls of our lovely Farnese.

FRANCESCO BORGIA:

Could the people see as well as that?

LUCREZIA:

We were all sitting high up in the choir on both sides of the altar.

THE POPE:

No, children, that's not it! You can laugh and joke all you want, wear pearls and eat candy. But there were Dominicans in that crowd, Florentines from Saint Mark's, disciples of Savonarola, our little troublemaker. They're the ones that stir our people up with the nonsense they prattle and with their wild eyes.

DON GIOFFRE:

Why don't we just chase the tramps away?

FRANCESCO BORGIA:

They're on mission here. They're conferring with their General.

DON GIOVANNI:

Oh, ho, and have we already come to such a sad pass that our ladies' jewels can be torn from their bodies, thrown into a bonfire and burned up?

DON GIOFFRE:

How much longer will Your Holiness continue to take orders from the ass of Florence?

THE POPE (*winking*):

We have invited him. He doesn't come.

DON GIOVANNI:

> You mean he refuses to obey?

THE POPE:

> Medici protects him. Lorenzo has grown penitent.
> He inquires daily of Savonarola about his prospects
> in Heaven.

LUCREZIA:

> Who is Savonarola, *Santo Papa?*

THE POPE:

> He's someone who won't let you eat candy or wear
> pearls.

> *Laughter.*

DON GIOFFRE:

> There must be some way! . . . Has the Church run
> out of poison?

CESARE (*darkly, sharply*):

> Later!

> *A group of nobles to the extreme right as seen from the stage.*

FIRST NOBLEMAN (*whispering*):

> You know that the Duke of Bisaglie was found in
> the Tiber last night?

SECOND NOBLEMAN:

> Yes, he drowned.

THIRD NOBLEMAN:

> Yes, and with three deep stab wounds in his back!

FIRST NOBLEMAN:

> He must have been really drunk to leave the
> Vatican at night. . . .

THIRD NOBLEMAN:

It is always dangerous to leave the Vatican at night, drunk or not drunk . . . and especially if you are the husband of our lovely Lucrezia.

SECOND NOBLEMAN:

You mean? . . .

THIRD NOBLEMAN:

I mean that the Duke of Bisaglie was strangled last night in the presence of his wife Lucrezia and her brother, Don Cesare!

First and Second Noblemen give a start of surprise.

SECOND NOBLEMAN:

But the stab wounds?

THIRD NOBLEMAN:

They came from an attack four weeks ago. A band of masked gentlemen fell on him in front of Saint Peter's. The Duke had the effrontery not to die.

Both again start with alarm.

FIRST NOBLEMAN:

But look at Lucrezia! She's as happy as a bride on her wedding day.

THIRD NOBLEMAN:

Lucrezia is a child! His Holiness made her Princess of Nepi this morning and sent her a basket of candy.

SECOND NOBLEMAN:

And does the Pope know?

THIRD NOBLEMAN:

Alexander the Sixth knows nothing! Rodrigo Borgia knows all.

FIRST NOBLEMAN:

And what will he do?

THIRD NOBLEMAN:

He will say a mass for the peace of the soul of the Duke who fell into the Tiber, and he will inform the Prince of Ferrara that Lucrezia is free.

The sound of music comes from the back of the stage. The three noblemen separate. In the background couples can be seen dancing. Meanwhile the table is cleared and taken away. The entire company sits or reclines on stools and cushions. The groups do not remain motionless. People stand up, go from one to the other, chat, drink, taste the sweets that are served, return to their places. In the interval a few of the dancing couples pause. Some of the ladies, warm and flushed, come toward the front of the stage. The Pope seizes a basket from one of the servants, takes sweets from it, and tosses them between the ladies' breasts. There is merry laughter both from below and from the gallery above. The music has stopped playing.

THE POPE:

Where are our *buffoni* hiding out? Tell them to come in! As for us, we shall sit here. (*He points to the left where there are seats. To Lucrezia*): Come, child!

Pulcinello enters with Colombina and his troupe. They give a mime show. Pulcinello wears a white costume with a leather belt, a ruffled collar, pointed cap, and a black half mask; he holds a harlequin's wooden sword in his hand. With much

bowing and scraping, grimaces and contortions, he begins by
addressing the public. Suddenly he tries to strangle himself,
holding his hands as if they belonged to someone else. He
moans and groans, pretending to die. Colombina comes
forward from the rear, can't bear what she sees, pretends to
be frightened and covers her face with her hands. The Pope
understands the allusion and shakes his finger at them.
Thereupon they stop and the real play begins: Colombina is
the young wife of old Pantalone; she is carried off by
Pulcinello and the husband is deceived. Constant peals of
laughter during the play and lively conversation.

THE POPE (*during the play, speaks caressingly to Lucrezia, who is*
sitting on a cushion at his feet):
Today is really a sad day for you, my darling. Your
wonderful Duke died so suddenly.

LUCREZIA (*childlike*):
Yes, he fell into the Tiber.

THE POPE (*with sympathy*):
Were you very fond of him?

LUCREZIA (*as above*):
Oh, yes, very fond!

THE POPE:
Don't be upset. We've already found you another.

LUCREZIA (*with lively interest*):
Is he as handsome as my Duke?

THE POPE:
Much better, my love.

In the play Colombina and Pulcinello loudly kiss each other
behind Pantalone. The latter, turning around suddenly, gets

a volley of powder in his face and proceeds to stumble around with no one coming to his assistance. His plight is greeted with loud laughter on all sides. The Master of Ceremonies, Burcard, enters and walks toward the Pope.

BURCARD (*to the Pope*):

Your Holiness, Vespers have begun in the chapel. The Church is packed to capacity. The people are awaiting your Easter blessing.

THE POPE:

But we want to see the play. Besides, the death of our beloved son-in-law has caused us a sudden shock. (*Pointing to the gallery*) Open those windows and tell the people that I shall attend Vespers from the loggia up there.

The Master of Ceremonies leaves.

Immediately afterward, between the arches of the gallery above, where the people are standing, one sees the windows open backward from inside the church. Friezes and entablatures of columns, statues and lighted candles become visible. Meanwhile the play continues. Pulcinello, holding his wooden sword, pursues and beats Pantalone, who runs back and forth in confusion. Colombina hides behind Pulcinello and follows in his steps. Suddenly one can hear, coming through the windows over the gallery, the many voices of a Gradual sung in a melancholy and tragic key.

CHORUS:

De profundis clamavi ad te Domine; Domine exaudi vocem meam; Fiant aures tuae intendentes in vocem deprecationis meae; Si iniquitates observaveris Domine, quis sustinebit? Speravit anima mea in Domino, a custodia matutina usque ad

noctem; quia apud Dominum misericordia et co-
piosa apud eum redemptio. Et ipse redimet nos ex
omnibus iniquitatibus nostris.[1]

*At the very first notes of the Gradual the people in the gallery
draw back in awe from the windows and, making the sign of
the Cross, turn halfway toward the interior of the church.
Below, one can see, somewhat in the background, a few
embarrassed faces. The Pope and his family, however,
continue to be merry, and the play goes on. The atmosphere
has become somewhat constrained.*

*Shortly after the Gradual the play also ends. The Pope
gives a sign to the musicians, who strike up another number
to which couples begin to dance in the background. Pulcinello
and his troupe take their departure with deep bows and
grotesque capers. The guests throw gold pieces to them. The
Pope beckons Colombina to him, strokes her cheeks, and
presses an additional piece of gold into her hand. She kisses
his hand and departs.*

THE POPE (*clapping his hands after the music has stopped*):
Now where are our lovelies?

(*This is the sign for a curtain to open at the back of the
gallery and twelve exceptionally beautiful Courtesans, clothed
only in light, transparent veils, cross the hall and take their
places to the right at the front of the stage. The Pope, ladies,
and gentlemen go up to them, examine them critically, and
welcome them with an exchange of jokes and small talk.*)

---

[1] I called out of the depths, O Lord, to You; Lord hear my voice;
Let Your ears hear the voice of my supplication; If You, Lord,
will count our sins, who will stand such a test? My soul waits on
the Lord from morning watch to night; for in the Lord is mercy
and in Him is full redemption. He will redeem us from all our
sins.

THE POPE (*with surprise after examining all of them*):
Where is Pignaccia? [2]

ONE OF THE GIRLS (*while the others remain silently embarrassed*):
She went to Naples . . . to Charles.[3]

THE POPE:
What? Are you too going over to our enemies?

(*The Pope and his company again draw back to the left, where, as before, they form groups on stools and cushions. Lucrezia sits on her father's lap. He fondles her. Servants place the large, three-branched, brightly lit candelabra, which previously stood on the table, on the floor in the middle of the hall. There is hand clapping. This is a sign for the girls to throw off their veils. Servants of the Pope, standing behind the ladies and gentlemen, now take chestnuts from baskets and throw them over the heads of the spectators into the middle of the hall. The girls rush for them and scuffle over them. Loud laughter. A circle forms around the girls, who are struggling on the floor.*

From the gallery as well, where in the meantime the people have crowded back, loud laughter resounds. As soon as a supply of chestnuts has been gathered, the courtesans arrange them carefully in a pile to the right near their clothing. Then fresh chestnuts are thrown and the struggle begins over again. One of the girls, whose hair has come undone, comes too close to one of the candelabra and catches on fire. The Pope jumps up, letting Lucrezia slide to the floor, and puts out the fire with his robe.)

---

[2] A famous hetaera of the time, who was later executed.
[3] Charles VIII of France, who, shortly before, had taken Naples.

THE POPE (*when it becomes clear that the girl has suffered no harm, slapping her gently with his hand*):
You rascal! That could have started you on your way to Purgatory!

Laughter.

THE COURTESAN:
Oh, you wouldn't have let me burn in Purgatory any longer than you did here, *Santo Papa!*

More laughter, in which the Pope shares.
    When the chestnuts have all been gathered up, they are counted and each girl is given a prize according to the number of chestnuts she has collected. The music begins again, and the servants pass around refreshments. There is loud conversation throughout the hall, especially concerning the charms of the girls. As the music comes to a stop:

THE POPE (*clapping his hands again*):
And now send the athletes in!

On the other side of the gallery two naked, strong men enter from behind a curtain. They are led to the girls, the sight of whom excites them. Then, as another signal is given, they begin to wrestle.[4] The spectators crowd around the wrestlers, urging them on and applauding. Even the girls follow the contest with the greatest interest. After the victor has thrown his opponent amid great applause, he walks over to the courtesans, chooses the most beautiful girl, and, as the spectators laugh and joke, leaves the hall with her. The loser leaves alone.

[4] These spectacles at the Court of Alexander VI were called *battaglie d'amore*, Battles of Love.

*At this point a second pair enters the hall. Excitement
among the spectators continues to mount. Applause,
expressions of approval, suggestions fly about as interest and
passion increase. As a fifth wrestler, amid loud cries and
applause, throws his opponent and also claims his choice,
there sounds forth from inside the church, in deepest, tragic
tones, the closing song of Vespers:*

Veni sancte Spiritus
Et emitte coelitus
Lucis tuae radium.
Veni pater pauperum
Veni dator munerum
Veni lumen cordium
Sine tuo nomine
Nihil est in homine,
Nihil est innoxium.
Lava quod est sordidum,
Riga quod est aridum,
Sana quod est saucium.
O lux beatissima
Reple cordis intima
Tuorum Fidelium[5]

*A painful stillness comes over the scene after the first notes.
Once more the people in the gallery stand back fearfully in
order to make room before the windows. Some of those present
leave the hall. Meanwhile the sixth wrestler with his partner*

[5] Come, Holy Spirit, and send the ray of your heavenly light.
Come, Father of the poor, giver of goods, light of our hearts.
Without your light, men are nothing, empty, burdened with sin.
Wash us clean of sin; refresh those that are dry; and heal the
wounded. O most blessed light, fill the hearts of your faithful!

*the show to continue. His family and intimates watch the
show, but manifest their annoyance at the disturbance. This
continues until the seventh wrestler has taken his departure to
the accompaniment of the church music.*

*After the end of this last match, the atmosphere becomes
somewhat more enthusiastic and interest is livelier. Once
more the circle closes around the wrestlers. In the church the
lights go out and the windows are closed from within. The
show still continues.*

*During the ninth match a messenger rushes into the hall
and whispers excitedly to the people standing in the rear. The
excitement spreads to the front rows. Cries are heard:*
"What's the matter?" "What's wrong?"

RODRIGO BORGIA (*Captain of the Pope's Guard*):

The King of France, Your Holiness, is on his way
from Naples and is marching on Rome! He is only
a few miles away!

THE POPE (*starting up, excitedly*):

The devil! To Orvieto! The Spaniards and Cata-
lans come with us! Take our strongboxes and
valuables! Forget the baggage and the mules! We'll
all go by horse! Pallavicini will stay as Governor of
the City with some of the troops. He will receive the
King with all due honor, but he will also threaten
him with excommunication, in our name, as a
disobedient son of the Church if he should remain
more than twenty-four hours in our territory.
Cesare will cover our march. And don't forget the
Church gold! Come! Let's go!

All leave in great confusion.

THE CURTAIN FALLS

ACT THREE

$\mathfrak{S}$CENE 1

In Heaven. An intimate council room in blue. A substitute throne, comfortable and plain. God the Father, Mary, Christ, the Devil. The first three are seated. The Devil stands before them, leaning on one foot and supporting the other with his hands. He wears a black close-fitting costume, is very slender, close-shaven with a fine-cut face, but his features wear an expression that is decadent, worn, embittered. He has a yellowish complexion. His manners recall those of a Jew of high breeding. He leans on one foot; the other is drawn up. He stands erect.

GOD THE FATHER (*serious and to the point*):
My friend, the reason We sent for you . . . a very special mission is involved . . . (*He hesitates*) . . . which calls for a certain dexterity. . . . I am aware of your intellectual gifts . . .

(*The Devil bows.*)

. . . and I just wonder . . . (*He hesitates*) . . . What is involved is, uh . . . a being, uh . . . a thing, which . . . uh, an influence, which might just conceivably be able to restore to the path of virtue . . . uh, and to true decency . . . that disgusting and abandoned humanity that craves . . .

(*The Devil makes a courtly gesture of sympathy and inner understanding.*)

. . . What I'm thinking of is some sort of punishment they will really feel . . . uh, so that . . . uh . . . (*turning to Christ*) My dear Son, You tell him. Words don't come easily to Me. I've always been one to act. I've never put much stock in words.

CHRIST (*rising with difficulty, thinking for a moment, then speaking easily*):
Sir! . . . It occurred to Us to turn to you for help . . . in a matter . . . which may prove to be to our mutual advantage. . . . I do not mean to imply— and I say this explicitly at the outset in order to avoid any possible misunderstanding—that you would in any way relinquish your claim over mankind in the earthly sphere.

(*The Devil makes a gesture of understanding and protest, as if to say that the thought had never occurred to him.*)

On the contrary, you would have even more complete control over this sphere than before. What is involved is a compromise, an agreement, a readjustment of the boundaries of our previously defined, reciprocal powers, without any loss of authority for either of the contracting parties, whereby your unimpeachable skill, your acuity, your tact, your indulgent cooperativeness, your culture, your . . . your . . .

He begins to cough, breathes with difficulty, moans and pants. His throat rattles. His eyes bulge. His brow is covered with sweat. He is going into an asthma attack.

MARY (*springing forward while the Devil feigns with great elegance a discreet embarrassment*):

Take it easy, Son. You shouldn't try to talk. It only makes You worse. After all, You're sick. (*Turning to the Devil with complicity*) My dear friend, We need your help—and it won't be at all necessary for anyone to know that you had anything to do with it.

(*The Devil protests reassuringly.*)

Come on, give us a hand. You won't regret it. (*She winks at him.*) You know what I mean.

(*She points to God, meaning that He's deaf, old, and feeble and cannot be an obstacle. The Devil bows.*)

Now, in plain language, here's the situation. Someone (*she points to the Old Man*) took it into his head, most regrettably I must say, to show Us a little scene that occurred in the Pope's Palace in Rome . . . in his rooms. What's that Pope's name, anyway?

THE DEVIL (*very cooperative*):

Ah, Alexander the Sixth, Rodrigo Borgia.

MARY:

That's it, Borgia. . . . Oh, and what a scandal it was. Ghastly! And at Easter Communion!

GOD THE FATHER (*suddenly bursting into unrestrained vulgarity*):

Ugh! Devil's filth! Ugh! Devil's filth! Ugh! Devil's filth!

CHRIST (*stirring from his lethargy and agreeing in a dull voice*):

Yes, Devil's filth! Ugh! Devil's filth!

THE DEVIL (*in great confusion, annoyed, disturbed*):
> You will forgive me . . . under the circumstances
> . . . I must decline . . . it becomes impossible . . .

(He takes a step backward and is about to withdraw.)

GOD THE FATHER (*turning to the Devil in a conciliatory tone*):
> For God's sake, no! I didn't mean you . . .

THE DEVIL (*offended*):
> It was my impression . . .

GOD THE FATHER:
> No, no! . . . A thousand times no! It's not true! It
> just slipped out . . . an old habit . . . I forgot . . .

THE DEVIL (*returning, elegant, conciliatory, with a bitter smile,
flicking a bit of dust from a sleeve*):
> Please . . . please . . .

MARY:

> No, no, my friend, you're one of Us. There can be
> no question about that. And no question of differ-
> ences. We need you far too much. (*Directing her
> words loudly and pointedly to the Old Man*) We shall
> never allow Our dearest cousin, Our ally, Our
> dearly beloved brother . . . to be insulted.

(The Devil bows courteously.)

> Now, to make a long story short, here's where we
> stand: It has been contemplated in high places
> (*pointing to God*) that it would be just as well to
> destroy the entire human race. This idea, however,
> has now been abandoned because of more impor-
> tant considerations, and we now prefer a more
> conventional type of revenge. Something old-fash-

ioned . . . along the lines of the Flood or Original Sin. That's why we consequently need someone, something, an influence, a force, a person, a disease, some little thing that will put a stop to the lewdness of humanity, especially of the Neapolitans and Romans . . . from a sexual point of view. Oh! You know what I mean! (*She pours a little cologne onto her handkerchief and holds it to her nose, breathes in slightly, while making eyes at the Devil over the handkerchief.*) Something that will call a halt to the bestiality of all those males and females who seem to be quite unaware that contact and penetration are purely incidental and to be tolerated only within the absolute limits of the needs of reproduction. Oh, it's unbearable! (*Breathes in more cologne.*) Surely you see what I mean!

THE DEVIL (*in a deep bass, somewhat stagy*):
I see what You mean.

GOD THE FATHER (*roaring*):
Yes, yes! Put a stop to it!

CHRIST (*with the voice of a consumptive*):
Yes, yes! Put a stop to it!

THE DEVIL (*after reflection*):
I presume it should be something quite painful?

MARY (*extending her lace handkerchief toward the Devil and nodding vigorously; speaking as if for the two others as well as for herself*):
Exactly. It should be very painful.

GOD THE FATHER (*looking on glassily, seeming not to understand, groaning finally in agreement in a thick, rasping voice*):
Yes, yes!

CHRIST (*still in attack, recovering slowly, breathing heavily*):
Yes, yes!

THE DEVIL (*standing with head bowed in thought, two fingers against his lips*):
Should this thing follow as an immediate consequence?

MARY:
Of course! Of course it should!

GOD THE FATHER (*still staring glassily*):
Of course! Of course!

Christ tries to repeat, "Of course! Of course!" but is too slow and breaks into Mary's following speech. Mary pays no attention and continues, waving her handkerchief to silence her Son. The latter follows her every movement with greedy eyes.

MARY (*to the Devil*):
You're on the right track, my friend. Oh, I can see that We're going to be very pleased.

The Devil gives Mary a short, sharp glance, then sinks again into his thoughts. After a long pause, during which only the throat-rattle of Christ is audible, he speaks.

THE DEVIL (*emphasizing and accenting his words in a way of his own*):
Well, then, we'll have to put the sting, the disease, uh, the something . . . (*raising his finger as if taking aim*) . . . into the thing itself . . . into the . . . hm! (*clearing his throat as if to make a point*) . . . into the contact!

MARY (*very worldly*):

Lovely! Perfectly lovely!

GOD THE FATHER (*not understanding, looks on with staring, bulging eyes. He reproduces the intonation rather than the sense of Mary's words*):

Yes, yes, yes.

Christ also tries to imitate, but can't get the words out. He becomes alarmed at his own predicament, stares first at God the Father, then at Mary. He finally produces a rhythmical, inarticulate "Ah! Ah! Ah!"

THE DEVIL (*after observing Christ's effort with a cool stare, yet without interrupting his own thoughts, continues with emphasis*):

We should introduce the infection into the secretion at the moment of sexual union.

MARY:

Oh? What do you mean? Oh, but that is very interesting! (*Sits up straight on her chair.*)

God the Father and Christ, who seem to have understood this time, sit staring goggle-eyed at the Devil.

THE DEVIL (*repeating the thought he has just had, as if to fix it in his own mind*):

We should introduce the infection into the secretion at the moment of sexual union.

MARY:

You mean the seed? (*She holds her handkerchief for a moment before her mouth as if she were trying to swallow something unpleasant.*)

THE DEVIL (*interrupting*):

No, no! Not the seed! Not the egg! Otherwise the children would be affected, and once they've been corrupted and made aware, we'll have had it! No, they must not be allowed to escape! We must leave the seed and egg alone so that human procreation can go merrily on. What we must find is some small by-product that will infect the aggressor as he plunges ahead, driven by instinct; something that will appear simultaneously with seed and egg and, as with snakes, is equally harmful to both parties, both partners in the game of sex—forgive me if my words offend—

(*Mary raises her eyebrows to indicate that she has understood.*)

so that the man can infect the woman or the woman the man, or, more ideally, both can infect each other, thoroughly unaware, completely caught up in their frenzy, in the fraud of total happiness.

(*He makes a gesture with his hand, as if to ask Mary if she has understood. Mary responds with delight, waving her handkerchief to say that she had indeed understood.*)

Babbling like babies, they'll rush blindfolded into the whole hideous mess!!!

MARY:

It's glorious! It's charming! It's diabolical! But how will you ever do it?

God the Father and Christ continue to stare goggle-eyed.

THE DEVIL:
> Ah, Madam, that will be my problem.

MARY:
> Very well, but only under one condition. Whatever you do, mankind must continue to have need of redemption.

THE DEVIL (*with great self-control*):
> Mankind will always remain in need of redemption.

MARY:
> And mankind must always remain capable of redemption.

THE DEVIL (*raising his arms, like a salesman, to shoulder height*):
> Capable of redemption! After I've polluted them! And to order yet! That's asking a lot!

MARY (*springing down from her throne and retreating hastily in the direction of God the Father and Christ*):
> In that case it's all off! If We can't redeem mankind any more, then what's the point?

> (*God the Father and Christ raise their hands in despair. Christ, who is somewhat better, begins now to follow with more lively interest.*
> *The Devil turns on his right heel, smiles sardonically, and shrugs his shoulders. He feigns regret. Very much the Jewish merchant. A painful moment. The deal seems to be off. Pause.*)

MARY (*returning slowly to her throne in order to divert their attention, suddenly asking the Devil in a friendly voice*):
> By the way, how's your foot?

THE DEVIL (*playing her game*):

Oh, so-so! No better! But no worse, actually! Oh, god! (*Hitting his shorter leg a blow.*) There's no change any more! Blasted thing!

MARY (*in a lower voice*):

Your fall did that?

(*The Devil, not reacting, is silent for a while; then he nods gravely.*)

(*Very cordially*) Well, anyway, how's Grandma?

THE DEVIL (*equally cordially*):

Lilith? Oh, thank You, very well!

MARY:

And the little ones?

THE DEVIL:

Thank You, thank You! They're fine.

Another pause. Mary, undecided, goes finally over to God the Father, with whom she speaks for a moment in a low voice. Thereupon . . .

GOD THE FATHER (*obviously having received instructions*):

Come now, my friend, you should be able to think up something that will hurt humanity without destroying it completely! Then, afterwards, We'll redeem it again! Won't We, My Son?

CHRIST:

We'll redeem humanity again!

MARY:

We've got to redeem humanity again!

THE DEVIL:

> The assignment is too difficult! I'm supposed to find something that is disgusting, amusing, and lethal at the same time! Then I'm supposed to get at them directly, violently, in their secret, amorous relationships and poison them right there on the spot! If those are the conditions, then the soul has got to be a part of the deal! That's where the soul is!

GOD THE FATHER (*surprised*):

> That's where the soul is?

CHRIST (*also surprised, but repeating mechanically*):

> That's where the soul is?

MARY (*affirmatively, half to herself, as if she were remembering*):

> That's where the soul is. . . .

THE DEVIL (*to God, after a pause, rather sarcastically*):

> My God, You're the Creator, aren't You? You ought to know!

GOD THE FATHER (*reluctantly*):

> We . . . uh . . . no longer create. We are tired. Besides, the area of earth and sense lies in your sphere. So make up your mind! Defile the soul if you must, but it must remain redeemable.

CHRIST (*still weak, attempting to repeat after God, but getting only as far as*):

> Defile . . . the . . . soul . . .

THE DEVIL (*to God the Father*):

> It should make them want to make love, You say, but at the same time act as a poison?

GOD THE FATHER:

> Naturally, otherwise you won't catch them!

CHRIST (*breathing again*):
> Passion . . . makes . . . them . . . blind.

MARY:
> Well, if you want to catch mice, don't use pepper.

GOD THE FATHER:
> Stick your nose into your witches' kettles! You'll find plenty of stuff! That Hell of yours is well supplied with everything! You're a good cook when it comes to stews like that! Stir it up! Mix it up! Create! Whip up something!

MARY:
> At all events, it should be something very seductive. If possible, something feminine.

CHRIST:
> Yes, something very seductive.

THE DEVIL (*following a train of thought*):
> Libidinous and destructive at the same time? And still not ultimately destructive to the soul?

ALL THREE (*at the same time and all together*):
> Libidinous! Destructive! Seductive! Lethal! Lustful! Horrible! Something to set the brain and blood on fire!

GOD THE FATHER:
> But not the Soul! Because of contrition! Because of despair!

THE DEVIL (*suddenly terminating his train of thought*):
> Stop! I've got something! I must have a word with Herodias! (*Half to himself*) Libidinous and destructive at the same time! (*Out loud*) I want to show you something!

MARY:
> The Lord be praised!

THE DEVIL (*turning to leave*):
> I think I've got it!

GOD THE FATHER:
> Bravo! Bravo!

MARY:
> Bravo! Bravo!

CHRIST:
> Bravo! Bravo!

ALL THREE (*delighted, rising as far as they are able*):
> Bravo, good Devil, bravo! Bravissimo!

THE DEVIL (*bidding them farewell and snapping his fingers as he leaves*):
> I'll be right back!

> *The Devil leaves. As he opens the door, he sees several younger angels outside who have been eavesdropping. He catches the nearest one by the wings and roughs him up. The angel runs off with the others amid frightful screams. One then sees the Devil open a trapdoor through which he descends, closing it after him. The three Divinities disappear into the right wings as the scene changes.*

$\mathbf{S}$CENE 2

Slowly the heavenly Council Room rises upward. The stage grows darker. The scene changes to a gloomy, barrel-shaped tunnel, wider at the bottom than at the top and constructed of gray stone blocks. Like the inside of a tower or a well, it seems to stretch backward into infinity. At the far end there is a rotten wooden staircase that has been frequently mended and is now barricaded off. Presently one sees the Devil coming down the stairs, not without difficulty, groaning and holding tight to the banister. At the same time he can still be seen from the set that is moving upward. Fantastic birds and monsters, some sitting on perches, some crouching in niches in the wall, hiss and croak a greeting to him with hoarse cries. This well-like passageway leads finally to a larger, dark, cellar-like room only partially illuminated by a reeking oil lamp and in which one can see at first, in the foreground, to the right, only a carelessly made bed of woven rushes. The oil lamp is on the other side and farther back. The Devil, tired and limping as he arrives, walks for a moment up and down, sighing, then goes to the back of the stage. One hears a heavy chest being opened. The Devil takes off his tight-fitting black suit and places it carefully in one of the compartments. He returns to the front of the stage wrapped in a warm coat made of animal skins patched together. He moans again, takes a few steps as if not knowing what to do. Finally he sits down on his bed, draws his feet up and plunges his hands into his thick hair, covering in this way his brow and the upper part of his face.

THE DEVIL (*to himself*):

So, you old dog, you! Back home again in your own place, squatting on your own bed! Forgotten and kicked downstairs! Dismissed! Audience finished! No family background? Then don't ask for any favors around here, young man! So you managed to get another peek at the fancy rooms of the High and Mighty? Well, you're still the clod, the pimp, the crook! Up there they can do just as they damn please! Anything they want! Nothing's low enough, cheap enough, dirty enough for the likes of them! Anything goes when you belong to the aristocracy! But who cares who you are or what you do? You could drill your way through to China with your own nose and you'd still be the low, filthy bum!

(*A pause while he reflects.*)

Just suppose now you were Royalty! That clubfoot of yours would be royal! Or suppose you were a doorman up there. Just a plain, common doorman! You'd have an angelic face and an angelic smile! You'd be celestial down to the rags you'd wear! But as things stand, you won't ever be anything except a dog! Oh, yes, if they want you to do something for them, something they can't do and that's really dirty, then they'll turn on the smiles and say, "My friend! My friend!" But once the audience is over, then back to your dirt and mud! Back to your "Devil's filth! Devil's filth!" from there on out! So make up your mind to it! You come from the dirt and you'll stay in the dirt! They'll grind you down and twist you around as long as you live! And you'll hobble along on that game leg of yours and eat crow as long as they cram it down your throat!

The Hell you say! You're better than they are and you know it! You're better than all those phonies lumped together! With their success and their houses up in the clouds! You belong to the real world! You've got thoughts inside your head! When you sit here alone, smelly and dirty, all of a sudden a light goes on inside your twisted brain and something jumps out that doesn't give a holy damn for all their despair! It's like a poison! Or a spark, a power that bounces and blasts across the world until it shatters the hollow heads of Heaven! You don't need any crowns to wear. You don't need ambrosia or champagne to drink! You don't need rings on your fingers and bells on your toes! You like things just as they are! You're happy! Happier than they can ever be! You like your hole in the ground, your precious tunnel! There's a smell of earth and spice down here, a smell of dirt that gives you strength! It produces thought and makes you work! Who gives a damn about their families and family trees! A clean slate! That's what you've got! A clean slate! You can afford to begin at the beginning! You don't have to sit around doing nothing! You can work! Let them keep their past! The future belongs to you! Work! Work! (*Jumps up.*) So, goddammit, let's get to work!

(*He walks up and down for a while, stopping now and then to think.*)

So what they want is something seductive. Naturally. It's got to be if you want to catch anything.

"Something feminine," Mary said. Very good! No one knows a woman better than Mary! But it must also act as a poison. That's where the punishment angle comes in. And they mustn't notice that it's poisonous! They must gulp it down like honey! Fine! Can be done! Now—body and soul must be contaminated in the process, but not permanently! Only to the point of "despair," only to the point of madness! Ha! I get the point! What they want is to watch! Watch them bend and break! Watch while they vomit up their souls like the contents of their stomachs! Still—you've got to be able to repair the soul! What is it they say? The soul must remain "capable of redemption"! Well, if all they want is to watch, I can give them that pleasure! But they didn't mention the body! Very good! As if you could separate the body from the soul! So—after I've polluted the body good and proper and the poor dope has just about gone to the Devil—Oop! Excuse me!—I mean, is just about ready to expire and the soul is well on its way to me, then that's when they want to redeem it! Divine Mercy, they call it! Well, we'll see!

(Again he walks silently up and down, reflecting.)

Now, just what kind of poison should it be? What is it that destroys and still doesn't destroy? Chemical or organic poisons are out! You can't proceed quantitatively! They would just drink the stuff down and ask for more since it's going to be so sweet! And then, whoops! There they'd be, stiff on their beds! There'd be no way to get the dosage

right. And I couldn't exactly leave a prescription on
their bedstands! No, it's got to be something
wonderful! Something quite unusual and completely new! Something slow-acting so that it won't
take effect right away! Something insidious that
spreads quietly and can always be found in a few
living specimens. And then the poison must involve
mankind's greatest pleasure, his sexual ecstasy, his
most costly, his most naïve delight! That way you
can be sure you'll get them all! Yes, but that was
exactly what I said! After all, intellectual property
is intellectual property! So all right. Where do we
go from here? Where am I supposed to find such a
poison?

(*Stands still, reflecting.*)

Of course! Naturally! In me! (*Cool.*) Is there
anything more poisonous, more physically penetrat-
ing than myself? Perfect! So now what? How'm I
supposed to manage that? (*Reflecting, speaking very
slowly, pointing with his index finger, as if dictating to
himself*) Since the poison may be too strong and
deadly in itself, you've got to dilute it organically
first and only subsequently introduce it into a living
being. (*Claps his hands.*) That's it! Now let's go over
that again. You must first make the thing organically so mild that their stomachs and livers can
stand it and at the same time give it reality through
the medium of a living being created in their own
image! Well, I'll be damned! And secondly, this
living being must be a woman; the poison has got to
be introduced through the usual body channels!

And thirdly, this woman must be lovely and I must be her father! Wow! (*Rubs his hands.*) And so there we are back to sex! Well, after all, they said create!

(*Walks excitedly up and down.*)

Now, if I do manage to bring this masterpiece off, just what is there in it for me? My friend, you'd better watch out! There won't ever be any second chance! Now's the time to make your demands if you ever mean to! (*Reflects.*) First, (*looking upward*) they've got to repair that staircase! It's a mess! If I should ever slip and break my foot, then I'd really be a cripple! And that trapdoor up there is a disgrace! God knows how many times I've bumped my head! I've got to have a nice free passageway with a railing and a couple of rugs. And I'm fed up with these so-called audiences! If they can come down here as they please, then I've got to be able to go up there as I please! I'm fed up with this business of giving advance notice! After all, He comes down here without giving any notice! Then (*very firmly*) this censorship stuff has got to stop! My books have got to be free to circulate in Heaven as well as on Earth! That must be an absolute condition! Otherwise I don't go to work! (*In an outburst.*) It's an outrage not to be able to share your thoughts with others! What's so hard to understand about that? Why can't He grasp the simple fact that there's real pleasure, a real joy in communicating your own thoughts to another mind? After all, you can take an awful lot of crap as long as you can communicate! So that's got to be Number One. Then, they've got to do something about this ventilation!

(*He stares at the ceiling for a moment.*)

Actually, I suppose I could have them put in some
gold moldings. Oh . . . it wouldn't improve the
light much. . . . I could ask Him to make me a
Count? Count Meraviglioso! Or just plain Italian
Conte di Meraviglioso. Signor Conte di Meraviglioso! Ugh! Shame on you! Didn't you say you
wanted to remain an honest man? Sure you did!
But you also wanted to experience for one little
moment the mad feeling of being something that
didn't require any justification! Just for a week.
Then you could turn it over to your substitute. . . .
Who knows? I might even manage a couple of
medals at the same time? No, it's too dark down
here. You wouldn't be able to see them. What else?
Well, I do need some clothes. I've been wearing this
Spanish stuff since Philip the Second. It's incredible! If I weren't so careful, I wouldn't even be able
to show my face upstairs! And then, for God's sake,
I've got to have some furniture! I should at least be
worth a sofa or two! And a couple of warm
blankets. Then what? Maybe even a little gold
braid? The rank of Lieutenant? And a recognized
place in Court! Even if it's in the lower ranks! Good
God, after all, I'm a big help to those people! Then,
if I get my title, maybe I could have a little angel or
two in keeping with my position? It would be a real
pleasure to have one of those cute little creatures
around here! I wouldn't care how skinny or young
it was, I'd fix that! And then what? A gold sword?
The title of Chamberlain? A little crown? A Duke's
frill or . . .

(He suddenly stops, covers his face with his two hands and screams like an animal.)

Ah! Ah! Keep away! *(He holds out his hands as if to fend something off and draws back.)* Ah! It's coming! It's got me! You dog! You knew it would get you if you went too far! Devil's filth! Devil's filth! *(He spits and seems to be about to throw up.)* Ugh! Devil's filth! It's coming! The Nausea! It's got me! Ugh! Ugh! It's too late! The Nausea! The Nausea! Ugh! The taste! So you forgot, Devil? You forgot how to starve, how to live without light, how to suffer? Do you still think you're so grand now? Ah! Ah!

(He chokes and retches, drags himself to his bed, throws himself face downward, writhes, tears some straw from his mattress, rolls it into a ball and stuffs it into his mouth with both rage and relief. Gradually he becomes calmer, lies motionless on his bed and seems to fall asleep. There is a long pause.

Now the back of the stage begins to grow light. The separating curtain becomes transparent. A seemingly unlimited perspective is revealed. Gradually the last opaque veil disappears. A huge Field of the Dead becomes visible. An almost inconceivable number of figures, apparently all women, are lying there as if asleep. They wear pale robes. Some are crouching. Some lie outstretched. Some lean on their arms. Some conceal their faces in their folded arms. A cold, flickering light floods the scene like moonlight. There is a deep stillness.

The Devil slowly awakes, raises himself feebly with both hands. As he turns and catches sight of the scene, he suddenly rises to a sitting position and snatches the ball of straw from his mouth.)

THE DEVIL:

Ah! You got here faster than I did! (*He contemplates the scene at length with delight.*) So you've come to life, my sweet dreams! It was the bad ones that crawled into my stomach and made me sick. That's as it should be. If you want to get well, you pay the price!

(*He lies down again, still somewhat exhausted, but now in a more comfortable position. He keeps the whole scene before his eyes. He speaks feebly and with difficulty.*)

Which one shall I choose to be the mother of my glorious child? Lovely! Seductive! Sensual! Poisonous! Something to burn the brain and blood! Unaware! Depraved! Cruel! Ruthless! Vile! Naïve!

(*Long pause. He rises to a sitting position and calls out gently, softly, but clearly.*)

Helen! Helen of Troy! Lover of Paris! Trojan Queen!

(*At the back of the stage a figure rises slowly from among the sleeping women. She wears a long, flowing gown that is gathered at the waist by a cord of the same color. She advances slowly, as if she were sleepwalking, with closed eyes. She walks in a shimmering light that accompanies her out of the Realm of the Dead. She comes forward and stands before the Devil.*)

THE DEVIL:

A long time ago you ran away with a young lad, a Trojan Prince. You abandoned your husband, the King. Was it because you were in love?

(*With difficulty Helen shakes her head no.*)

What? Not even in love? Then it was out of curiosity?

(*She seems to think for a moment. Then, still asleep, she nods affirmatively.*)

Just for the fun of it?

(*Helen nods.*)

You didn't think anything in particular?

(*She nods.*)

And when the War broke out, what did you think?

(*She nods without thinking. Then, upon reflection, shakes her head no.*)

Did you think: that's the way things go?

(*Helen nods affirmatively and with emphasis.*)

Go on! Go back! Go back to sleep, poor, simple thing!

(*She waits for a moment, then turns slowly and returns to her place.*
  After a pause, the Devil speaks in the same clear, soft voice.)

Phryne! Phryne of Athens! Loveliest hetaera of them all! Come out!

(*A woman, dressed the same as the first, rises from another group on the Field of the Dead and comes forward.*)

White sorceress! You caught a thousand men in your net! You made them poor and miserable! You took their money and their minds! You made fools out of philosophers! You made justice corrupt! You made a mockery of the law! You started wars! You amassed wealth! You behaved like a goddess! You were worshiped! You scoffed at your country! For the sake of your obscene publicity, you wanted your name cut in the walls of Thebes! You were even ready to pay for it! You showed yourself naked to the people! You erected temples and statues to yourself in Corinth! You were a whore until your hair turned white! And finally, like an unclean animal, you were slaughtered in a temple where you had taken refuge!

(*She nods affirmatively in silence at the Devil's words.*)

Why? Out of love?

(*She shakes her head no.*)

Out of passion?

(*She shakes her head no.*)

For kicks?

(*She nods affirmatively.*)

Because you were lovelier, whiter than all the rest?

(*She nods affirmatively.*)

You didn't think about anything?

(*She shakes her head no.*)

You just let things take their course?

(*She nods affirmatively.*)

You can go. You're harmless! You're innocent!

(*She leaves, slowly and silently, like the first.
   The Devil continues after a short pause.*)

Héloïse! Abbess of Paraclet! Latinist of the twelfth
century!

(*A third figure rises on the Field of the Dead and comes
forward. She is dressed like the others.*)

You were a student. You were a lover. You were the
mother of children. You seduced your teacher,
Abelard, the light of his century. You brought your
family to scorn and shame. Finally they made a
eunuch of your lover and of you a nun! And still
you went on loving your Abelard, castrated or not.
You wrote him letters full of fire! Then they made
an Abbess out of you. But even the Abbess studied
and loved her lover more and more! In her
imagination she gave him children! She committed
such abominations with her frigid friend as cannot
be told even in Hell! You wrote to him: Better to be
the whore of Abelard than the lawful wife of the

King! Then he died, and you had his body brought to you. You loved him still so much that you dug his grave and buried him with your own hands! And then for twenty more years you exhausted your imagination loving him! Until you too died!

(*Héloïse nods to all of his statements.*)

Tell me, why? Out of love?

(*She nods emphatically.*)

Go, my child! You're ripe for Heaven! Be ready! You'll be the first when the trumpet calls! But while you wait, sleep on, sleep on!

(*The Figure leaves. The Devil speaks to himself.*)

Damned slim pickings in Hell! I mean, if you want something really outstanding. But there must be some good monsters around here! (*Pauses to reflect for a moment.*) Agrippina! Mother, wife, and murderess of Kings! Agrippina! Murdered by a King! Agrippina! I'm calling you!

(*A figure arises out of another group.*)

Your record is one of the best, Agrippina! You were married at fourteen and after nine years you were good enough to bear your husband a child! It was Nero! The greatest monster of them all! Oh, it wasn't your fault! Don't be alarmed! We have a school now that can prove that nothing is anyone's fault! The only trouble is that Heaven hasn't heard

about it yet! And so you left your husband and
went with Lepidus. That's the way they did things
in those days! Then you plotted with your suitor to
murder your brother, Caligula, the Emperor. It
didn't work out. Oh, but it wasn't your fault! You
just didn't quite have the touch! But finally Caligula did manage to get himself killed. Things like
that happened in those days. And so you could
show your face again! Then you tried to catch a few
other prominent Romans, but you had a streak of
bad luck. Until, of course, the wealthy Passimus,
the Advocate, condescended to a second marriage. I
would never have thought he was such a fool! You
poisoned him and became his heiress. Nothing
unusual about that. Plenty of others had done as
much before. Things like that happened in those
days! But I must say, your next little bit had real
originality! You managed pretty well behind the
curtains of that villa! You got the Emperor, Claudius, to slash the throat of his own wife, Messalina!
Then you married Claudius and you became the
Empress! The rest was just a matter of detail: the
suicide of Lucius Silanus—you engineered that; the
banishment of his sister, Junia, and of Lollia
Paulina. You had their heads brought to you as an
afterthought! You were only following the trend of
the times! Then you assumed the name Augusta,
"The Holy," and made Claudius adopt your son!
Next you married Nero to the sister of Claudius,
Octavia. Then you poisoned your own husband and
proclaimed your son, Nero, Emperor! Now I call
that something new! Subsequently you poisoned a
few consuls, proconsuls, rivals, and ultimately you
were murdered by your own son!

(*The Figure has responded to all statements by nodding in silence.*)

So now listen to me, Agrippina! You are a very charming person. But what I miss in everything you have done is the true artistic drive! The authentic naïveté! Everything about you comes from limitless ambition! That's not healthy! In the final analysis it's a bore! That's not the way we work these days. Not one single aesthetic murder in your entire past! Honestly, I don't see how I can use you. Go on! Go back to sleep! And sweet dreams!

(*To himself after a moment of thought*) I've got just one number left. Herodias! But now let's see! Why not take the daughter instead of the mother? (*He calls*) Salome! Graceful, lovely, beautiful dancer! Salome! Come out!

(*Far to the back of the stage a slender, youthful apparition rises and comes forward. On her face is an expression as if she were remembering something extremely pleasant.*)

Tell me, pretty child, you were at Herod's banquet?

(*She nods affirmatively.*)

You danced, didn't you?

(*She nods.*)

Why?

(*She doesn't know.*)

Was it because pretty young girls always like to dance? And because you had taken dancing lessons?

(*She nods.*)

Everyone applauded?

(*She nods.*)

And so Herod said you could name your gift?

(*She nods.*)

So you said you wanted a head?

(*She nods.*)

A man's head?

(*She nods.*)

A real man's head that was still alive?

(*She nods.*)

Why?

(*She doesn't know.*)

For a toy?

(*She hesitates and finally nods affirmatively.*)

So Herod sent you into the prison with the hangman and there he cut you a head?

(*She nods.*)

It happened to be the head of John the Baptist?

(*She nods indifferently.*)

They laid it on a platter and you brought it back into the banquet room?

(*She nods.*)

The blood ran into the platter until the platter was full?

(*She nods.*)

You got your fingers wet?

(*She nods vigorously.*)

Did you like that or didn't you?

(*She nods yes.*)

What do you mean, yes? Did you like it or didn't you?

(*She rubs her hands together.*)

You mean you got a kick out of it?

(*Her affirmation is very clear.*)

You must have very sensitive fingers!

(*No answer.*)

And then, then you gave the head to your mother as a gift?

(*She nods.*)

Why?

(*She shrugs.*)

It was already dead?

(*She nods sadly.*)

But you wanted a head that was still alive?

(*She nods.*)

Yes, amputated heads don't last very long! Now, tell me, did you care about any of those people? Was there anyone that you loved?

(*She doesn't know what to say and finally shakes her head no.*)

Did you love Herod?

(*No.*)

Saint John?

(*No.*)

Your mother?

(*She shrugs, then shakes her head no.*)

But you did like your sliced-off head?

(*She nods yes very definitely.
    The Devil suddenly jumps up.*)

You're it, my child! (*Goes over to her.*) I can use you!
(*He takes her gently in his arms, standing a little behind
her.*) You follow me. We're going to my bedroom.

*One hears the Figure moan deeply and distinctly.
    During the following scene black veils and shadows fall
over the Field of the Dead and over the front of the stage. At
first they are transparent. Then gradually the whole stage
darkens.*

THE DEVIL (*leaving with the Figure to the right and speaking softly*):
We have great things to do together, you and I!
You will be the mother of a magnificent race which
no aristocracy will ever equal. Your children won't
have blue blood or red blood in their veins. It will
be a far more remarkable kind of blood! You're the
only one of your kind in my whole, huge realm!
Even up there, at Court, they watch us benevo-
lently and wish us well!

(He disappears with her. His voice sounds farther and farther away.)

By tomorrow you will be back among your companions. With our hot blood we'll finish our work of creation in no time at all! Come, child, come!

Now the Field of the Dead has disappeared. The veils fall thicker and thicker over the front of the stage. Soon there is complete darkness. In the distance one hears a sharp woman's cry. Now it is deep night.

THE CURTAIN FALLS

Act Four

*In Heaven. An expensively decorated rose-colored room.
Mary is sumptuously dressed and is sitting on her throne.
She is surrounded by angels, most of them young. Their
clothing is lightweight and of many colors. Some sit on the
steps of the throne; some lounge about in artistic poses. One of
them is holding a book and is reading aloud from Boccaccio
in a monotonous, painstaking, schoolgirl voice.*

ANGEL (*reading*):

". . . Agilulf, King of the Lombards, secured his
throne, as his ancestors had done in Pavia, capital
of Lombardy, by marrying Teudolinga, the widow
of Auterich, who had also been King of the
Lombards. The bride was very beautiful, clever and
honorable. One of her admirers, however, played
her a very bad trick. When the State of Lombardy
was once more peaceful and happy, thanks to the
valor and cleverness of King Agilulf, it so happened
that one of the Queen's grooms, a man of very
humble circumstances as far as his origins were
concerned, yet now raised far above his lowly
calling, handsome as to his person and as tall as the
King, fell desperately in love with the Queen. Since
his humble state in no way prevented him from
understanding that his love lay outside the boundaries of all reason and all hope, he spoke of his
feelings, like the sensible man he was, to no one and

did not dare reveal himself even to the Queen by the slightest glance. Although he was now completely without hope, he nonetheless took pride in the fact that his intentions were so exalted, and, afire with love, he made every effort to outdo his comrades in all things that he thought might be pleasing to the Queen. It came about, consequently, that the Queen, when she went out riding, invariably preferred the horse which this groom held to any other. He, meanwhile, counting this as a supreme favor, stood close to the Queen's stirrup and was happy if he managed but to touch her dress. As we often observe, however, that love grows stronger in proportion as hope diminishes . . ."

MARY (*interrupting*):

Yes, yes! But haven't they managed to get together yet?

ANGEL (*no longer reading*):

I don't know, Eternal Virgin.

MARY:

See how many more pages there are!

ANGEL (*counting carefully*):

Twenty, Most Blessed Mother of God.

MARY:

But that's endless! Can't you skip something? (*Takes the book.*) . . . Oh! . . . This looks better! . . . Go on! Go on reading! (*She returns the book.*)

ANGEL (*reading*):

". . . As we often observe, however, that love grows stronger in proportion as hope diminishes, it so happened that the poor groom, who could no longer endure his secret longing unalleviated by any hope, and who was by now a prisoner of his love, took the resolve to die. . . ."

At this moment the Woman crosses the threshold of the door timidly. She is a young, blooming creature with black hair and deep black eyes in which a smoldering sensuality, as yet only half awakened, is apparent. She wears a white veil. All rise. All are thunderstruck and nearly blinded by the newcomer. The angels stand motionless, as if not knowing what to do. All eyes are glued to the Woman.

MARY (*who has risen and who now speaks imperiously*):
Who is this person?

(*There is no answer.*)

Who let you in? Where do you come from? Are you from . . . down there? Are you dead? Or are you something better than dead? Are you a Saint by any chance? What do you want here? Is this meant to be some kind of competition for me? I must say you've got a lot of nerve! (*She begins to tremble with anger.*)

At this moment the Devil enters behind the Woman. He is out of breath, as if he had been hurrying to keep an appointment. He bows deeply before Mary.

THE DEVIL:
Madam (*presenting the Woman*), my daughter!

The angels rush offstage, to the left, screaming.

MARY (*descending the steps of the throne, wearing an expression of deepest amazement*):

Oh! . . .

THE DEVIL (*waiting for the effect to sink in; then after a pause*):

I hope you like her?

MARY (*hesitating, assembling her thoughts*):

Like her? No indeed! She's far too pretty for that! That little beast is going to make us all look silly. . . . In Heaven or on earth! I expected a horror!

THE DEVIL:

Madam, allow me . . .

MARY (*interrupting him and flying into a temper*):

Madam! Madam! Will you please remember that I am the Eternal Virgin and the Most Holy Mother of God! . . . Now don't forget it! (*With a glance at the Woman.*)

THE DEVIL (*sanctimoniously and in a low voice*):

As yet she doesn't understand these fine distinctions. She is still a child.

MARY:

You mean she doesn't talk?

THE DEVIL:

God save us!

MARY:

She doesn't speak any language?

THE DEVIL:

She speaks the language that every woman speaks! The burning language of seduction!

MARY:

> Don't you think you've gone too far? Haven't you pushed our program just a little bit? We didn't quite need all of this! What is this marvelous creature supposed to do?

THE DEVIL:

> I had to give her some kind of . . . form!

MARY (*interrupting him*):

> Well, if I had wanted that sort of thing, I could have sent one of my angels! I could even have gone myself!

THE DEVIL:

> Oh, never, never! Most lovely Lady! You have forgotten . . .

MARY:

> Yes, yes! Of course. You're right. But was it absolutely necessary to make her so blinding? She's sheer enchantment! (*In a low voice and turning toward the Devil*) Are we going to have to worry about what she thinks?

THE DEVIL:

> Feel perfectly free! She won't think anything. Her mind's a blank!

Mary devours the Woman with her eyes. Then, on a sudden impulse, goes over to her and kisses her. The Woman recoils, almost as if she were afraid.

MARY (*overwhelmed*):

> Sheer enchantment! Just like a child!

THE DEVIL (*with comic emphasis*):
"Straight from the hands of the Creator!"

MARY (*getting the point*):
Oh, a little joke! Tell me, where did you get her?

THE DEVIL (*boastful*):
We can't give away any professional secrets. But I can tell you the name of her mother.

MARY:
Ah?

THE DEVIL:
Salome! The lovely head-hunter! She danced so prettily that she won first prize! It was a human head . . . still warm!

MARY (*thinking*):
Don't we have her up here somewhere?

THE DEVIL (*sharply*):
No, no! You don't have people like that up here!

MARY (*fascinated by the Woman*):
. . . . You don't have people like *that* up here! And so dazzling!

THE DEVIL:
The visible part of her comes from her mother.

MARY:
From her, of course.

THE DEVIL (*sarcastically*):
But the invisible part . . .

MARY (*looking at him and understanding his meaning*):
I see what you mean! You mean . . .

THE DEVIL:

> Her father's qualities will emerge later. After she's had a little practice.

MARY:

> I can believe you.

THE DEVIL:

> I was never in better form!

MARY (*who can't take her eyes off the Woman*):

> So that's what you intend to poison and destroy humanity with? With that enchanting innocence! With those eyes! With the impact of that unearthly appeal! With that superhuman goodness and compassion!

THE DEVIL (*firmly*):

> I do indeed!

MARY:

> You do? . . . But can you?

THE DEVIL (*sneering*):

> Can I? Let me tell you. . . . The poison that runs through those veins is so strong that anyone who touches her will have eyes like glass marbles inside of two weeks! Their brains will liquefy and they'll gasp for hope like fish out of water gasping for air! In a matter of six weeks they won't recognize their own bodies! Their hair will fall out! Their eyelashes will fall out! Their teeth will fall out! They won't be able to chew, and their joints will be sprung! Inside of three months their entire body surface will look like a sieve and they'll go out window-shopping to see the new styles in human skins! And don't think

that the fear will remain only inside their hearts! The stench of it will seep out through their noses, and their friends will exchange glances, and the ones that are in the first phase of the disease will laugh at those who are in the third or fourth! A year later their noses will fall into their soup, and then it'll be the rubber-goods department for a new one! Then they'll move, go to some new place, get a new job. They'll become sympathetic and sentimental. They'll be kind to animals and develop a moral sense! They'll play with flies in the sunlight, and they'll be envious of the young trees in the spring! They'll turn Catholic if they're Protestants, and Protestant if they're Catholics! After a couple of years their livers and glands will feel like cement inside their bodies, and they'll want light food. Then one eye will begin to smart, and in another three or four months it'll be closed! In another five or six years they'll begin to shake and have shooting pains! It'll feel like fireworks going off! They'll still be able to go out walking, but they'll keep turning around, patiently, to see if their feet are keeping up with them! A little later they'll prefer to lie in bed—because of the warmth! Then, one fine day, after about eight years, they'll be able to pick one of their own bones right out of their bodies! They'll smell it and then they'll throw it, in horror, right across the room! That's when they'll start getting religious! Religious, religious, and more religious! They'll begin to like books with leather bindings, very tooled, with lots of gold leaf! . . . And a cross! . . . And so there they'll be, on their beds, ten years later, nice and slim, all dried up, skeletons, with their mouths open, yawning at the ceiling! And

they'll say, "Why? Why?" And then they'll die!
. . . And then, then . . . you'll get the soul!

MARY (*turning away in disgust*):
Ugh!

THE DEVIL (*surprised*):
What's the matter? Haven't I done what I was
supposed to do? Isn't that what you ordered?

MARY (*with her hands over her face*):
Oh! The poor creatures! The poor creatures!

THE DEVIL (*interrupting*):
. . . will remain in need of redemption and capable of redemption!

*Mary has now turned around and is again lost in
contemplation of the Woman. The latter, thoroughly
unaware, retains her original, naïve pose of eloquent beauty.
One hears offstage the sound of approaching footsteps.*

MARY (*coming to herself and going quickly to the door*):
No! Don't let anyone in! (*As she sees who is there*) No!
My Son cannot come in! He should not come in!
He may not come in! (*Returning, frantic*) Get that
woman out of the house! I don't care what you do
with her, but get her out! This minute!

THE DEVIL (*imploring*):
Dear Mary, Eternal Virgin, Most Holy Mother of
God! Just one or two little requests! . . . Please!
I've earned something! . . . You promised!

MARY (*in a hurry*):
Yes, yes! You'll get your staircase! But now clear
out! Get her out of here!

THE DEVIL (*almost in tears*):
>   And freedom of thought!

MARY:

>   You already think far too much, my friend! But
>   we'll see! Now get out!

>   *The Devil bows deeply before Mary, gives a heavy sigh,
>   then, with an air of dignity, as if aware of his high position,
>   accompanies the Woman to the exit. He lets her go first.
>   Mary stares at the departing couple with open mouth.*

THE CURTAIN FALLS

Act Five

＄CENE 1

*Rome. A hall in the Papal Palace. To the right (as seen
from the stage) a temporary altar has been set up against the
wall. Before it a priest is officiating. On the left and reaching
to the center of the stage, there are armchairs. Some are
equipped with prayer stools. The Pope and his family are
seated. Among the latter are Cesare and Lucrezia Borgia,
Vanozza, Julia Farnese; there are also members of the
College of Cardinals, Bishops, Archbishops, Almoners, the
Master of Ceremonies, Burcard; the Captain of the Pope's
Guard, and others of the immediate followers of the Pope. To
the extreme left, behind the chairs and blocking the view of
the hall on this side, a thick crowd of ecclesiastics and lower
officials of the Pope's Court. Completely to the rear of the
stage there are a few servants who follow the holy ceremony
with varying degrees of attention. The only light in the whole
room comes from four tall candles that are burning on the
altar so that the farthest corners of the stage are shrouded in
darkness. To the rear is a large, single door, which stands
open.*

PRIEST AT THE ALTAR (*who has been moving about and whispering
for some time*):
Hoc est enim Corpus meum.

(*The whispering continues.*)

Hic est enim Calix Sanguinis mei, novi et aeterni testamenti, mysterium fidei, qui pro vobis et pro multis effundetur in remissionem peccatorum.

(*To all appearances indifferent, the Pope sits with crossed legs and hands folded in his lap. Around him are the spectators, some of whom are kneeling, others standing. Among the rest, especially the women, there is lively conversation. The exchanges of remarks are constantly interrupted by discreet sounds of* "Pst!" *coming from those at the rear.*)

Hostiam puram, hostiam sanctam, hostiam immaculatam . . .

(*Taking candy from a bag, Lucrezia passes it around to her younger brothers and sisters.*)

Panem sanctum vitae aeternae, et Calicem salutis perpetuae. . . .

(*The youngsters fight for the candy. They rush to pick up the pieces as they fall. There is the sound of scuffling and scolding. Chairs are pushed about. The women fuss over the children. The men call for order. The Pope looks up and smiles. From the rear one hears repeatedly the sound of* "Pst! Pst!"
    The Priest continues in the same voice.)

Per omnia saecula saeculorum.

THE SPECTATORS (*mechanically*):
    Amen.

*Cesare gets up, goes over to the chair of his father, the Pope,
leans down and speaks with him at length in a low voice.
The women begin to chat with each other again in low tones.
The children, now quiet, chew on their candy.*

PRIEST AT THE ALTAR (*in a low voice*):
Agnus dei, qui tollis peccata mundi . . .

(*As these words are spoken, the Woman suddenly enters
through the door at the rear of the stage. Behind her a black
figure can be seen disappearing. She has the same bearing as
in the previous scene in Heaven, naïve and enchanting. She
wears the same veil, which seems to give off an illumination
independent of the light from the candles.*)

. . . miserere nobis!

(*Immediately there is great confusion and agitation among
the spectators, whose eyes are glued to the door. The room is
filled with an inextricable mixture of cries of surprise and
admiration from the men, of imprecations from the women.
    The Priest continues in a low voice.*)

Agnus dei, qui tollis peccata mundi, miserere nobis!

(*The confusion increases. The Captain of the Guard takes a
few steps toward the door. The servants press more and more
toward the center of the stage.*)

Agnus dei, qui tollis peccata mundi, dona nobis
pacem. . . .

(*The Pope has now also risen and stands staring at the door,
where the Woman remains, serenely poised. Groups form and*

*talk excitedly. The Master of Ceremonies, Burcard, comes
forward in order to look after the Pope. The latter pays no
attention to him. The children scream.*
    The Priest concludes.)

Dominus vobiscum!

The response "Et cum spiritu tuo" *cannot be heard.*
    Now cries arise from all sides. "Who is she?" "Where
does she come from?" "She's from Naples!" "Throw
her out!" "Stop! Stop!" *The voice of the Pope can be
heard, saying,* "Peace! Peace!"

PRIEST AT THE ALTAR (*turning around, dismayed by the confusion,
but concluding nonetheless*):
    Ite missa est! (*He gives the benediction, but no one pays
    any attention.*)

*Now all leave their seats and press toward the door. The men
first, then the women, the latter as if resisting, but carried
along by the crowd. The Pope, surrounded by his son,
Cesare, his Master of Ceremonies, and the Captain of the
Guard, leads the Woman in a courtly gesture of welcome
toward the center of the hall, while the men push forward
and the women scream their imprecations. Meanwhile, the
Priest has genuflected before the altar and has taken his
departure to the right. A sacristan arrives and extinguishes
the four tall candles. In the resulting half light, in which the
Woman seems to shine as if magically illuminated, one can
see the men rush wildly at the shining Figure, whom the
Pope now holds fast by the arm. The Captain of the Guard
has drawn his sword. Burcard raises his powerful arms high
above his head as a sign of warning. Cesare, in a rage,
strikes out blindly with his fists at the crowd. The prayer*

stools are overturned. Here and there a dagger flashes. In the background one can hear the suffocating cries of women. "Help!" "It's not me!" "You've got the wrong one!" "To arms!" "Soldiers!" *One can hear Lucrezia's voice:* "Cesare! Cesare! *Mio Papa!* Help!" *Finally the group manages to push its way out the door with the Woman and the Pope in the center. The crowd rushes after them as if driven wild. The women leave, screaming, to the right and to the left.*

THE CURTAIN FALLS

§CENE 2

*A street in Rome before the Papal palace. It is dawn, cold,
wet, and dreary. On one corner a nearly burned-out,
flickering oil lamp. A deathly silence.*

*A door of the Papal palace opens softly and the Woman
appears. Her skirt is insecurely fastened. She covers her
half-bare breast to protect herself against the cold. Her hair
is disheveled. She has the hollow eyes of a person who has
spent the night out and has not had enough sleep. She closes
the door softly behind her. She takes a few shuffling steps.
She is wearing two unmatching slippers, both too large for
her. She wears also diamond earrings and a diamond
necklace. She looks around timidly and cautiously.*

*The Devil jumps out at her. He has been standing in the
shadow of a gutter.*

THE DEVIL (*in a domineering voice*):

Now to the Cardinals! Then to the Archbishops!
Then to the Nuncios! First to the Nuncios of the
Italian States! Then to the foreign Ambassadors!
Then to the Camerlingo! Then to the Pope's
nephews! Then to the Bishops! Then to the monas-
teries! Then to the rest of the human pack! In that
order! Now get going! And don't forget who's boss!

Slowly the Woman leaves.

THE CURTAIN FALLS

⚙SKAR 𝔓ANIZZA'S 𝔇EFENSE

OSKAR PANIZZA:

My defense in the case of *The Council of Love* before the Royal Court of Munich I on April 30, 1895.[1]

> The concept of God: a hoax.
> The concept of morality: a hoax.
> —Nietzsche, *Antichrist*

Gentlemen of the Jury,

Since I am not a lawyer, I cannot express an opinion concerning the procedures, and more specifically the authority, of a German court in this case. I know from private

---

[1] The following defense was not in all respects, and not always literally, spoken as it stands here and as it was previously written. The proceedings, which required that the case be heard by the judge in the morning and answered by the district attorney in the afternoon, forced the defense to divide its arguments. Finally, to sum up the whole matter again in the presence of the jury was a hopeless task. Thus the part concerning Parny was left out. Other considerations, that arose extemporaneously, were twisted and have not been included

expressions of opinion by eminent jurists competent to judge in these matters that they hold completely contradictory views. I have been told that in this case there has been a violation of a clearly worded article in the German Penal Code which states specifically that an act occurring in a foreign country, and legal in that country, cannot be prosecuted in the home country. My attorney will address himself to this point. Meanwhile I can speak only of the human, artistic, and aesthetic aspects of this case. And since you, gentlemen, likewise are not lawyers and likewise are called upon to judge the human aspects of this case, I believe that we shall not be far apart at the outset of our deliberations and that it will not take us long to come to an understanding.

I think, therefore, that I shall best be able to explain my intentions in writing the play which is here under consideration if I tell you briefly how I came upon its subject matter.

You know, gentlemen, that toward the end of the fifteenth century in Italy, and later in Germany, there arose an illness which assumed epidemic proportions and which caused the most dreadful destruction to the human body. Apparently it was not transmitted originally through sexual contact but only later came to be spread almost exclusively through sexual intercourse, attacking all levels of society both high and low; it was called "syphilis." No one knew whence it came, but the impression it made on people's minds was enormous. The chronicles of the times are full of frightening descriptions of the ravages it caused to both mind and body. There was no cure, nor was there any escape. In a sense it was worse than the "black death." In the latter case the course of the contagion was known, and it

here. However, the sense and wording of the major portion of the utterances of the above communication correspond to what was said in the courtroom. (Panizza.)

was possible to escape to countries that had not yet been contaminated. But here was a malady that sprang up everywhere at the same time. Now, it inevitably happens that when a natural cause is not known, a supernatural cause is invented. Thus the people of those times came to believe that "syphilis" was a punishment decreed by God. Since they promptly discovered the relationship between the illness and sexual intercourse, they reasoned as follows: God's punishment had come as a consequence of human debauchery and sexual excess. Hence the German name *Lustseuche* (the disease of lust). We find the following passage from the year 1519 in a chronicler who was one of the most prominent personalities of his time, a militant writer and a poet, who also wrote a book on syphilis, Ulrich von Hutten: "It has pleased God in our time to send illnesses which, as far as we can tell, were unknown to our ancestors. Thus speak those charged with the defense of Holy Writ, saying that syphilis came from God's wrath, and so does God punish and afflict our evil ways." I have used this passage as an epigraph to my book in order to indicate from the start what I was about: namely, that I did not intend anything either blasphemous or lewd, but that I wanted to understand the particular situation of the people of those times, a situation which, since I was formerly a physician, was naturally of special interest to me.

Now consider, gentlemen, the position of a man who starts from this point, with full knowledge of the outcome of this dreadful disease, and who, in his attempt to explain the facts historically, stumbles onto the remarkable discovery that precisely the court where the worst sexual excesses occurred was the Papal court and that the personage who participated in the most incredible fashion in the wildest orgies was Pope Alexander VI—and this in spite of the fact that a short distance away, in Florence, there lived a man of the stature of Savonarola who preached atonement and day after day made the Pope aware of his depraved life! Now consider further that this same Pope, who like all of his kind is filled with a sense of his divinity, whose name is "Son of God," "Vicar of Christ," "God on Earth," "who is in direct contact with God in Heaven," is not reluctant to hand out Cardinals' hats to pimps, publicly keeps three mistresses in Rome, and finally has Savonarola hanged in order to be rid of this embarrassing preacher who had refused a Cardinal's appointment! And all of this while the horrible malady rages throughout Italy and while the common people, as well as scholars and theologians, go on saying that it is a scourge sent by God in his wrath as a punishment because of a lack of chastity among mankind! Meanwhile, there sits on Saint Peter's throne as Pope, as the head of all Christendom, a man who according to Roman teaching "receives his orders directly from God," and who is the worst of all offenders, about whom it is almost laughable to use the words "lack of chastity." [2] If you come now down to our own

[2] In the scene in which I describe one of the regular evening entertainments of the Pope, I had naked young men appear on the stage. They engaged in wrestling matches before the Pope and his ladies. The winner received as a prize one of the attending naked courtesans and disappeared with her behind the scene. Historical fact, however, is far, far worse. I toned down the scene, not out of consideration for the Popes nor because of the feelings of Catholics, but for reasons of artistic restraint. I did this because I had written with the theater in mind, hoping that a production of the play would be possible and because, if certain precautions were taken, the above-mentioned scene would become at least conceivable theaterwise. The real scene, as it comes down to us from history, would have been impossible even in a closet drama. According to the report of the Papal Master of Ceremonies, Burcard, which is confirmed by the dispatches of emissaries stopping in Rome, the original scene goes as follows:

"In sero (dominica, ultima mensis octobris, vigilia omnium sanctorum)—
October 31, 1501—fecerunt cenam cum duce Valentinense in camera sua, in
palatio apostolico, quinquaginta meretrices honeste, cortegiane nuncupate,
que post cenam coreaverunt cum servitoribus et aliis ibidem existentibus,
primo in vestibus suis; deinde nude. Post cenam posita fuerunt candelabra
communia mense in candelis ardentibus per terram, et projecta ante
candelabra per terram castanee quas meretrices ipse super manibus et
pedibus, nude, candelabra pertranscentes, colligebant, Papa, duce et G.
Lucretia, sorore sua presentibus et aspicientibus. Tandem exposita dona
ultima, diploides de serico, paria caligarum, bireta et alia pro illis qui
pluries dictas meretrices carnaliter agnoscerent; que fuerunt ibidem in aula
publice carnaliter tractate arbitrio presentium, dona distributa victoribus."
(Burchardi [sic] Diarium (1483–1506), ed. L. Thuasne, Vol. III, p.
167. Paris 1885). "On the evening of October 31, on All Saints'
Eve, fifty whores of high standing, known as courtesans, were
having dinner in the apartments of the Duke of Valentinois,
Cesare Borgia, son of the Pope, in the Papal Palace; after dinner
they danced with the servants and with others present, first
clothed, then naked. When the tables were cleared, lighted
candelabra were placed on the floor and chestnuts were thrown
in front of them. The naked girls, going in and out among the
lights on hands and feet, gathered the chestnuts. The Pope, the
Duke, and his sister, Donna Lucrezia, were present as spectators.
Finally prizes were displayed, silken garments, footwear, head-
gear, etc., which were to be awarded to those who would prove
themselves capable of having the most frequent sexual intercourse with the girls. By the decision of all those present sexual
intercourse was then performed with the latter, on the spot and
in full view. Prizes were distributed to the winners." The whole
business was a completely ordinary occurrence. The Venetian
emissary, Giustiani, sent forward the following report dated
December 30, 1502: "Yesterday I dined with His Holiness in the
Palace and remained until early morning to watch one of the
entertainments which are the regular diversion of the Pope and
in which young women take part, without whom the Pontifex
cannot conceive of any festivity. He has girls dance in His
presence every night and gives other parties of a similar nature
at which courtesans perform." (Yrarte, Ch., *Les Borgias.* Paris,
1889. Vol. II, p. 40)—NOTE BY PANIZZA.

times, where skepticism and nonbelief are rampant, and allow all of these historical coincidences and moments to fall as artistic material into the hands of a modern man who, unfortunately perhaps, has a bent for satire, then I ask you, gentlemen, how would you yourselves have described the Trinity and how would you have depicted the Gods in Heaven who, under such circumstances, were said to have sent "the disease of lust" across the earth as a punishment for mankind?

I should now like to examine this question from another point of view. At all times and among all peoples, gentlemen, attempts have always been made to bring the Divine into the realm of art and to portray it. And since in the portrayal of the highest and noblest things we must always resort to the experiences afforded by our own environment —we cannot know any other—painters, poets, and sculptors have always sought out their models for things divine from among earthly things. Dürer turned his madonnas into fair-haired German women; Murillo turned his into the fiery women of Spain; Dante in his great epic similarly peopled his transcendental spheres with Italians, and in the French mystery plays devils were endowed with Gallic temperament. And when an attempt was made to portray the Divine without regard for outward form, as did Klopstock, it remained caught in the abstractionism of purely conceptual form and mere verbalism. Now surely, gentlemen, you will not contradict me when I say that satire is as much a proper art form as any other, that *pathos* is as legitimate as *melos,* that the sock is as legitimate as the buskin! Now, if an author intends to write a satire, a satire or comedy of the Divine, he must, like any other artist, make use of human prototypes. He must carry over into the Divine the small grotesque traits that he has observed among men. I have shown above, sufficiently, I believe, that the outbreak of syphilis in the Western world, along with the attitude of the Pope and the judgments of contemporaries as to the causes of this divine punishment, was eminently satirical material. I have also shown the inevitable consequences of the Pope's conduct for a general concept of the Divine at large. In view of this, gentlemen, is there need for surprise that the portrayal of the Divine in *The Council of Love* turned out to be what in point of fact it is? I will confess, however, that the colors have been laid on strong.

You will perhaps, gentlemen, now make the following objection: the portrayal of the sublime in divine things is permissible, but the portrayal of the ridiculous is forbidden. I will concede this point. But you, gentlemen, on the other hand will concede that this cannot be the artist's point of view. If such a point of view had always been observed, not a single satire would ever have been penned. Neither of gods nor of men! For satire of men has always been much more severely punished than satire of gods. Lucian would never have written his *Dialogues of the Gods* or Aristophanes his comedies. The Englishman, Wright, would have been unable to compose his *History of Caricature*, as the German, Flögel, would have been unable to compose his *History of the Comic-Grotesque*. Notwithstanding, satire and *vis comica* have always been among the most powerful and beneficial resources in the realm of the mind. You have only to recall, during the time of the Reformation, the wide-ranging influence of Rabelais, whose brilliant wit served as a training ground for the mind and character of the French of today. His unbelievably indiscrete attacks on religion were actually published by permission of the king. Or recall the bold attacks on religion of the German satirical writers of the time of Fischart and Reuchlin. Perhaps, gentlemen, you will make one further objection: every artist must bear the

consequences in his own country of laws which govern his
artistic creation. That is correct, gentlemen, and it is for this
reason that I have appeared before you here. But you,
gentlemen, will perhaps grant my argument that satire is a
natural tendency rooted in human nature and that it
cannot be suppressed.

Gentlemen, our world today is not favorable to the
portrayal of the sublime in the sphere of religion. For
example, no one today can produce the colossal religious
paintings of a Hess or a Cornelius. Our times are more
inclined toward skepticism and criticism. For many this
may represent a step backward. Yet it was no different in an
earlier period. The Christian religion has often known
periods of the utmost skepticism, of the most profound
disbelief. It was then, especially, when the churches made
the most inordinate demands on men's hearts as well as on
their pocketbooks, that opposition and satire arose among
people of culture. Such a period occurred, for example, in
the first third of the eighteenth century in England when
the first Methodist communities were being founded. The
artist who attacked this period with the most irreverent
satire was the English caricaturist William Hogarth. I have
here one of his most famous engravings, which appeared
under the title of "Credulity, Superstition, and Fanaticism."
The scene represents the inside of a church. The service is in
progress. Below, among the devout—as if the artist wanted
to show the innermost thoughts of man—every sort of
sensual, lascivious, and suggestive abomination is taking
place, while above, from out of the pulpit, Holy Grace is
made an object of scorn in the most grotesque fashion. And
yet our own Lichtenberg, in his famous commentaries on
the engravings of Hogarth, states: "Mr. Walpole says of this
page of our great artist that it is the greatest example of
profound and useful satire which the latter ever produced.

Such praise is perhaps excessive; still it would seem that of all of Hogarth's engravings, this is the one that best deserves to hang in every home. The sight of it awakens horror and terror. Here everything is true." This small reproduction, which I shall pass among you, gives an excellent impression of the original. As chance would have it, it was produced and published here in Munich. Gentlemen, I have never heard that a Hogarth engraving was ever taken to court!

But, gentlemen, how tame the English appear where religious satire is involved when we compare them with our neighbors to the west, the frivolous French! The French Revolution was another of those periods when scorn for religion dared show its face in public. Previously there had been a long period of free thought. During the Revolution disaffection toward the clergy and the church increased immeasurably in the country of Voltaire; it became a kind of mania, and ultimately came to include all revealed religion; it was disaffection caused by a religion that simultaneously had been unable to prevent oppression and reduced the people to utter poverty. Hence arose the saying: *"Écrasez l'infâme." "L'infâme"* was Christianity. The expression originated with Frederick the Great in his correspondence with Voltaire. In the year 1799, gentlemen, there appeared, written by one of the leading poets of France, Parny, whom Voltaire called "the French Tibullus," one of the most libertine poems ever to have been written: *La Guerre des Dieux.* It caused an enormous sensation in France and was received with a storm of applause. It was thirty years before the poem was suppressed, and then only because the French had entered a period of reaction. Notwithstanding, it has been reprinted numerous times down to our own day and can be found anywhere in France as well as in our better bookstores here in Germany. In comparison with this poem, gentlemen, *The Council of Love* is a mere trifle. What is truly unscrupulous about this work is the fact that at no point does one ever clearly understand just why the gods are made to appear so implausibly ridiculous. And here, gentlemen, in my opinion, lies the difference between Parny's work and the work which has been submitted to your judgment. In my opinion, the artistic treatment in *The Council of Love* is completely justified by the nature of the subject matter, and the crassness of my portrayal is contained in the problem itself. Syphilis was something terrible in the Italy of those times. God had sent it as a punishment at a time when the Vicar of God was the worst libertine ever known to man, the worst in all of history. Parny's work is merely a superficial exercise of thought, frivolous wantonness, Gallic word play. In comparison with Parny, gentlemen, I can say confidently that my position is that of the moralist. Here briefly is an example of what I mean: the gods in Olympus are sitting together at a feast; spirits are running high; suddenly Mercury, the messenger of the gods, bursts in and announces: a race of new gods is approaching Olympus. Rage and consternation! A consultation is held to determine what can be done. Minerva, the goddess of wisdom, observes that in all probability the old gods have become increasingly meaningless and useless in the eyes of men. She expresses her fear of Jesus. Whereupon Jupiter says:

(Gentlemen, I must at this point beg your indulgence while I read aloud a few very strong passages, but they are necessary within the framework of this brief literary and historical survey which I beg you to follow.)

> "... *Fi donc! Ce pauvre diable,*
> *Fils d'un pigeon, nourri dans une étable*
> *Et mort en croix, serait Dieu?* ...
> *Le plaisant dieu!* ..."

("... Pooh! This poor fellow,
Son of a pigeon, raised in a stable,
And who died on a cross, is supposed to be
    God? ...
A funny god! ...")

Now Mercury is again sent off to take stock of the situation. He returns promptly with this information: Yes, it is true. The creatures who are presently ascending toward Heaven are in fact real gods. Once more rage and despair! The most outlandish proposals are now made, among them that they should all march out against the new gods and topple them out of Heaven. But Jupiter decides to make the best of a desperate situation. He sends out a messenger and, like a true Frenchman, invites them in to dinner. Now the Christian divinities come straggling in with their retinue of saints and sit down to eat with the gods of Olympus. The Trinity is represented by an infirm old man who holds a young lamb on his lap and has a dove on his shoulder. The lamb bleats, the dove coos; the old man tries to make a speech but cannot get out a single word; he laughs in embarrassment and finally sits down to eat!

> *"Une heure après les conviés arrivent.*
> *Etaient-ils trois, ou bien n'étaient-ils qu'un?*
> *Trois en un seul; vous comprenez, j'espère?*
> *Figurez-vous un vénérable père,*
> *Au front serein, à l'air un peu commun,*
> *Ni beau ni laid, assez vert pour son âge,*
> *Et bien assis sur le dos d'un nuage.*
> *Blanche est sa barbe; un cercle radieux*
> *S'arrondissait sur sa tête penchée:*
> *Un taffetas de la couleur des cieux*
> *Formait sa robe: à l'épaule attachée,*

Elle descend en plis nombreux et longs,
Et flotte encore par-delà ses talons.
De son bras droit à son bras gauche vole
Certain pigeon coiffé d'une auréole,
Qui de sa plume étalant la blancheur,
Se rengorgeait de l'air d'un orateur.
Sur ses genoux un bel agneau repose,
Portant au cou ruban couleur de rose,
Qui bien lavé, bien frais, bien délicat,
De l'auréole emprunte aussi l'éclat.
Ainsi parut le triple personnage.
En rougissant la Vierge le suivait,
Et sur les dieux accourus au passage
Son oeil modeste à peine se levait.
D'anges, de saints, une brillante escorte
Ferme la marche, et s'arrête à la porte.

L'Olympien à ses hôtes nouveaux
De compliment adresse quelques mots
Froids et polis. Le vénérable Sire
Veut riposter, ne trouve rien à dire,
S'incline, rit, et se place au banquet,
L'agneau bêla d'une façon gentille.
Mais le pigeon, l'esprit de la famille,
Ouvre le bec, et son divin fausset
A ces payens psalmodie un cantique
Allégorique, hébraïque, et mystique.
Tandis qu'il parle, avec étonnement
On se regarde; un murmure équivoque,
Un rire malin que chaque mot provoque,
Mal étouffé circule sourdement.
Le Saint-Esprit, qui pourtant n'est pas bête,
Rougit, se trouble, et tout court il s'arrête.
De longs 'bravos,' des battements de main,
Au même instant ébranlèrent la salle."

("An hour later the guests arrive.
Were there three of them or only one?
Three in one; you understand, I hope?
Picture in your mind a venerable father;
His brow is serene; he looks a little common,
Neither handsome nor ugly, rather spry for his age,
And firmly seated on the back of a cloud.
His beard is white; a radiant circle
Goes around his bowed head:
A piece of silk of the color of the sky
Is all his dress; pinned at the shoulder,
It falls in thick long folds
And continues to float beyond his feet.
From his right arm to his left there flies
A certain pigeon wearing a halo on his head;
Flaunting the whiteness of his plumage,
He gives himself the airs of a public speaker.
On his lap there lies a fine lamb,
He wears a rose-colored ribbon around his neck
He is freshly washed and dainty,
And shares the aura of the halo.
Thus appeared the personage that is three-in-one.
He was followed by the blushing Virgin;
As the gods crowded forward to watch her pass,
She barely raised her modest eyes.
A shining escort of angels and saints
Brought up the rear and stopped at the door.

To his new guests the Olympian
Pays his compliments
In a few cold, polite words. The venerable Sire
Tries to respond, finds nothing to say,
Bows, laughs, and takes his place at the feast.
The lamb bleats prettily.
But the pigeon, the family wit,

Opens his beak and his holy falsetto
Chants to these pagans a hymn
Allegorical, Hebraistical and mystical.
As he speaks, there is general surprise;
Glances are exchanged; there is a murmur of
    amusement;
Each word calls forth a snicker
That escapes and circulates in an undertone.
The Holy Ghost, who, after all, isn't stupid,
Blushes, becomes embarrassed, and suddenly falls
    silent.
Long shouts of 'bravo' and clapping of hands
Shake the hall at this moment.")

In the retinue of the Trinity come angels, saints, martyrs,
the Virgin Mary. The goddesses of Olympus find her dull
and gauche; her hair is badly done, and she is without chic.

"Fi donc! elle est sans grâce et sans tournure;
Quel air commun! Quelle sotte coiffure!"

("Ugh! She has no charm and her figure is bad!
How common she looks! How stupidly she wears
    her hair!")

The masculine inhabitants of Olympus find her, in spite
of a peasant quality in her prettiness, sufficiently attractive
so that they feel obliged to pay her court. They go over her
physical assets in a way which I should not like to repeat
here even in French. In this first canto, when dinner is over,
the new gods make a tour of the accommodations of
Olympus. Mary comes upon the dressing room of Venus. In
her curiosity she cannot resist trying on one of the sumptuous dresses that she finds there. At that very moment Apollo

appears. He is set on fire by the sight of this seductively dressed woman who promptly succumbs to the violent demands of the god of the Muses. I believe, gentlemen, that it will be a matter of indifference to you to learn the contents of the remaining nine cantos and that you have already come to the conclusion that we have here one of the most irresponsible works in all of French poetry. Further, it confirms what I have said previously: that the poet, when he depicts supernatural things, must always use the colors and forms of his own experience. Whether one paints the sublime or the ridiculous in religious subjects, the dress is always borrowed from earthly reality. In the works of Parny even Christian divinities speak and move in the manner of a French *salon* of the end of the last century.

Perhaps you will say, gentlemen, that the author of *The Council of Love* wants to re-establish himself in your eyes and so plays the moralist; he begs your pardon when he refrains from reading aloud a few perhaps even juicier fragments from the poem of some French author. No, gentlemen! In all conscience I make a distinction here between this French work and my own. I have deprecated the Christian gods, and I have done so intentionally because I have viewed them in the mirror of the fifteenth century and studied them through the glass of Pope Alexander VI. Gentlemen, our notions of the Divine are contained in our own thought. What in reality goes on up there you know as little of as I do. If our notions of the Divine are sublime, then they are sublime in our thought; if they are ridiculous, then they are ridiculous in our thought. Now, if someone should chance to appear, a dissolute Pope for example, and should happen to change our notions of the Divine from the sublime to the ridiculous, this would constitute a process that would occur in our thought and would have nothing to do with what really exists above us in space, in the transcendental world.

Thus, when I attacked the Divine, I did not attack the spark of the Supernatural that smolders in the heart of every human being, but I did attack the Divine as it became a caricature at the hands of Alexander VI.

Now, gentlemen, to refer again to our French author, perhaps you will make the following objection: In Germany such grotesque portrayals of the Divine have never occurred. Only the light-minded French or the disrespectful English have ever treated the Divine in such barbaric fashion. At the risk of keeping you a few moments longer, I must bring before you a sampling from the writings of the Swabian folk poet Sebastian Sailer (1714–1777), particularly from his comic drama *The Case of Lucifer*, which so greatly delighted Goethe. Here we enter a very different sphere, the sphere of Swabian folk poetry, but you will see that the coloration is the same. The first act begins with a chorus of angels:

> *"Danza, schpringa,*
> *pfeiffa, singa,*
> *seand im Himmel alte Ding;*
> *bei Schalmeia*
> *Juhui schreia.*
> *dasz oim schier der Sack verschpring.*
>
> *Hupfa, danza,*
> *d'Läus und d'Wanza*
> *über d'Schträhla schüttla ra,*
> *Schträhl und Kämpel*
> *naus zum Tempel*
> *wenn mar schreiet Hopsasa."*

("Dance, jump,
pipe, sing,
these are old things in Heaven;

to the pipes
yell: yoohoo,
until your belly bursts wide open.

Hop, dance,
your lice, your bedbugs,
shake them up with a curry-comb,
curry-comb and hair-comb
get out of the temple
when they yell: Hoop-la-la.")

The action of the play is as follows: Lucifer, the rebel of
Heaven, must be caught and brought before the tribunal of
God. This is finally managed. He is caught in a place which
one cannot mention in polite society. The Archangel
Michael shoots the bolt and Lucifer is a prisoner. The clown
Hanswurst lends a hand. Both hurry off to God the Father
to announce the news.

MICHAEL:

> *"Luschtig, Gott Vater! Ebbas Nuis!*
> *verschreaket itt, wenn ich mein Buffer aschuisz.*
> *Luzifer ischt g'fanga.*
> *Ich will nun gaun saga, wia's ischt ganga."*

("Courage, Father! I've got news!
Don't be afraid if I shoot off my gun.
We have caught Lucifer.
I will gladly tell you how it was done.")

They tell him, and God the Father rewards them with a
glass of wine.

GOD THE FATHER:

> *"Michel! gang in Kealler;*
> *doa hoascht Rheinwein, Muschkateller,*
> *Mosler, Neckarwein, Burgunder*

in di Flascha, ganze Plunder;
Velteliner und Tiroler
seand au guate Magasohler
wemma schpeit,
oder wenn dar Mag verheit.
Sag nun, was witt saufa?"

("Michael, go into the cellar;
There you will find Rhine wine, Muscatel aplenty,
Mosler, Neckar, Burgundy
In their bottles by the carloads;
The ones from the Valtelline and the Tirol
Will soothe your stomach
When you throw up,
Or when you have a bellyache.
Speak up, what will you drink?")

But the proffered wine is so sour that neither Saint
Michael nor Hanswurst can drink it. They decide that
Lucifer shall drink it as punishment for his countless
infamies. They ask God the Father for his approval.

GOD THE FATHER:

"Meinethalba, will's probira;
lasza g'schwind zua mar rein führa.
Hanswurscht! gang naus, suscht muasz ih lacha;
ih muasz gaun eanschtliche G'sichter macha."

("I don't care. I'll give it a try;
Have him brought to me, quick!
Hanswurst, get out! Or you'll make me laugh!
This requires a serious face.")

Now Lucifer is led in.

LUCIFER:

"Bardaun, Gott Vater, Bardaun!
Gealtat, ar kennat mich schaun?

GOD THE FATHER:

> *Wohl redle kenn dich,*
> *aber jetz b'sinn dich.*
> *Was hoascht ang'fanga?*
> *Wia weit bischt ganga?*

LUCIFER:

> *Bardaun, Gott Vater, Bardaun!*

GOD THE FATHER:

> *Halt's Maul! I kenn dich schaun.*
> *Sankt Michel hoat mer eaba gean an guata Roath,*
> *dasz da g'wis kommst in di graischt Noath.*
> *Gugg dötta as seall Glas Wein,*
> *vom Sai ischt as. Jetz glei trinks nein!*
> *Noah lasz ih für äll deine G'schpana*
> *an frischa raus lauffa uszam Hana,*
> *dasz ar wearat krumm und lahm uf älla Viera,*
> *oder müeszet gar wia d'Hund krebbieara."*

LUCIFER:

> ("Pardon, Father God, pardon!
> I'll bet you know me?

GOD THE FATHER:

> You just bet I know you.
> But now you listen to me.
> What have you been up to?
> How far have things gone?

LUCIFER:

> Pardon, Father God, pardon!

GOD THE FATHER:

> Shut up! I know you.
> Saint Michael has just given me a good bit of
>   advice

That'll surely get you into the deepest trouble.
Take a look at that glass of wine.
It comes from the lake. Now drink it down!
Now for all your comrades
I'll draw some more out of the spiggot,
So that you will crawl on all fours, twisted and
    lame,
Or so that you will die like dogs.")

But Lucifer refuses the wine. He knows, he says, where he
can find some that is better.

LUCIFER:

> "*Botz dausat Sakerment,*
> *und älle sieba Elament!*
> *Dar Duifel holl s'Michels sei G'schmoisz,*
> *dös wainsch ih, so wahr ih Luzifer hoisz.*"

> ("By a thousand sacraments,
> And all seven elements,
> The Devil take Saint Michael and all his tribe!
> This I wish him as sure as my name is Lucifer.")

Now God the Father orders the factious Devil to be thrown
into Hell.

MICHAEL:

> "*Maarsch, du Höllenhund, Maarsch!*

LUCIFER:

> *Leackat mar mitanand im Aarsch!*"

MICHAEL:

> ("Out, you Hell hound, out!

LUCIFER:

> All of you, kiss my ass!")

The Devil leaves. The remaining angels intone a hymn in praise of God.

You will observe, gentlemen, that this picture makes a very different sort of impression on us. In comparison with the exquisite, highly seasoned cuisine of Parny, here we have real German, Swabian fare! But, characteristically, whether German, French, or English, no people ever lets slip by the opportunity to satirize its own religion. And each makes use of the forms and colors of its own surroundings. And just as surely as Klopstock writes his *Messiad*, so does there arise out of the folkways of peoples an "Offenbachiad" of divine events intended to unleash our laughter. And what are the gargoyles and the grotesque animal figures that adorn the portals of our churches if not satires and comic epics in the religious domain?

Now who was this Sebastian Sailer? Some cheap wandering minstrel, perhaps, who would exchange off-color jokes for a few table crumbs or a glass of wine? Or perhaps a so-called eighteenth-century modern who hoped to make a name for himself with his daring literary work? Not at all! He was a famous clergyman–preacher, Canon of the Monastery of the Premonstrants of Obermarchthal in Swabia. His fame was so widespread that, as was the custom in those times, he took the pulpit throughout all of Germany, traveling as far as Franconia and Moravia, and even preaching in Vienna in the presence of the Empress. He was nicknamed "the Swabian Cicero." To be sure, he was frequently attacked because of his writings, and even the spiritual authorities were made to proceed against him. His superior, however, the Bishop of Constance, Cardinal von Rodt, went in person to Obermarchthal where, on the occasion of a tour of inspection, he asked to have one of his plays put on in his presence. His only comment was his applause. He did, however, brand the opinions of Sailer's opponents as wrong and stupid. Subsequently Sailer's writings were frequently published, and achieved in Würtemberg, as in the case of *Our Cousin from Swabia*, the rank of a beloved national saga. The edition, which I have before me, is illustrated by Nisle, the celebrated illustrator of Hebel. And in this scene which I have read to you, you can see Lucifer here in the costume of a Swabian village magistrate in top boots with large silver buttons and with his great wings pinned behind his back. Saint Michael is wearing a Bavarian military helmet and the uniform of a Napoleonic grenadier. God the Father is sitting in an armchair; he is wearing a flowered dressing gown, loose slippers over bare feet, on his head a nightcap with a crown of stars. Engraved on the back of the armchair is the so-called eye of God, the well-known symbol of the Trinity. Beside the chair stands a spittoon.

You see, gentlemen, humor and satire are two things in human nature that cannot be eradicated, and even in the religious domain they have their justification as they have their exaltation and their inspirational function.

Do you believe that today the times are such as to permit more rigorous censorship in this area? Gentlemen, half of a century has now passed since the appearance of *The Life of Jesus* by David Friedrich Strauss. You all know to what an extent this book, which has reached into the circles of all cultured people, has become, so to speak, a point of departure for religious skepticism in Germany. In our own times I need only mention the name of Harnack, whose book *The Apostolic Creed*, in which he rejects the supernatural birth of Christ as unhistorical, has circulated in some fifty editions throughout all of society. Also, gentlemen, even though I speak here before a group that is predominantly Catholic, you will nonetheless allow me as a Protestant to cite those instances which place my case in a somewhat different light from that in which it might appear in the eyes of a Catholic. You all know as well as I that today, throughout the German Empire, dozens of Protestant pastors have been suspended because in good conscience they could not pronounce the words of the baptismal sacrament as they have come down from the past and according to which Christ is said to have been born supernaturally. Meanwhile hundreds of other pastors are beating at the doors of the synods asking for redress and tolerance for this weak-faithed generation of ours. Do you believe, gentlemen, that at such a time it behooves us to summon religious satire before the courts, satire of a nature that already existed in earlier times?

Gentlemen, I appeal finally to your sense of fairness with respect to the country in which my book has appeared. This book was not published in Germany. It was published in Switzerland. Every German author has something to say that cannot be printed in Germany; he must consequently go abroad. English surgeons who wish to practice vivisection go to France, since vivisection is forbidden in England. When their work is finished they return home. It would never occur to any English court, however, to prosecute them, since the issue involved is legal in the foreign country. Now, if you treat a book published abroad, where it does not enter into conflict with the laws, as if it were published in the homeland, you pervert the intention of the author and place him in jeopardy in a situation where he cannot hope to defend himself. In other words, you do him a deliberate injustice. Gentlemen, I appeal to your innate sense of justice and ask that I be acquitted.

Plays Available in Viking Compass Editions

MAXIM GORKY:
> *Enemies* (C373) $1.95

SIMON GRAY:
> *Butley* (C372) $1.95

JOHN GUARE:
> *The House of Blue Leaves* (C353) $1.95

LILLIAN HELLMAN:
> *The Little Foxes* and *Another Part of the Forest:*
> Two Plays (C394) $2.95

JAMES JOYCE:
> *Exiles* (C84) $1.45

F. L. LUCAS (editor and translator):
> *Greek Tragedy and Comedy: Prometheus Bound,*
> *Agamemnon, Antigone, Oedipus the King, Hippolytus,*
> *The Bacchae, The Clouds,*
> and fragments of other plays (C227) $2.95

ARTHUR MILLER:
> *After the Fall* (C231) $1.45
> *The Crucible* (C157) $1.35
> *Death of a Salesman* (C32) $1.45
> *A View from the Bridge* (C73) $1.25

OSKAR PANIZZA:
> *The Council of Love* (C403) $2.95

DAVID RABE:
> *The Basic Training of Pavlo Hummel* and
> *Sticks and Bones:* Two Plays (C367) $2.25

PETER STONE and SHERMAN EDWARDS:
> *1776: A Musical Play* (C283) $2.45

HEATHCOTE WILLIAMS:
> *AC/DC* and *The Local Stigmatic:*
> Two Plays (C389) $2.45